Larger-Than-Life
LARA

Larger-Than-Life
LARA

Dandi Daley Mackall

Dutton Children's Books

DUTTON CHILDREN'S BOOKS
A division of Penguin Young Readers Group

Published by the Penguin Group
Penguin Group (USA) Inc., 375 Hudson Street, New York, New York 10014, U.S.A.
Penguin Group (Canada), 90 Eglinton Avenue East, Suite 700, Toronto, Ontario, Canada
M4P 2Y3 (a division of Pearson Penguin Canada Inc.) • Penguin Books Ltd, 80 Strand, London
WC2R 0RL, England • Penguin Ireland, 25 St Stephen's Green, Dublin 2, Ireland
(a division of Penguin Books Ltd) • Penguin Group (Australia), 250 Camberwell Road,
Camberwell, Victoria 3124, Australia (a division of Pearson Australia Group Pty Ltd)
Penguin Books India Pvt Ltd, 11 Community Centre, Panchsheel Park, New Delhi - 110 017, India
Penguin Group (NZ), Cnr Airborne and Rosedale Roads, Albany, Auckland 1310, New Zealand
(a division of Pearson New Zealand Ltd) • Penguin Books (South Africa) (Pty) Ltd,
24 Sturdee Avenue, Rosebank, Johannesburg 2196, South Africa • Penguin Books Ltd,
Registered Offices: 80 Strand, London WC2R 0RL, England

Library of Congress Cataloging-in-Publication Data

Mackall, Dandi Daley.
Larger-than-life Lara / Dandi Daley Mackall.—1st ed.   p. cm.
Summary: Using the writing techniques she has learned in school, fourth-grader Laney
relates how an obese girl new to the class changes the lives of those around her,
despite being bullied by her peers.
ISBN 0-525-47726-8 (hardcover)
[1. Authorship—Fiction. 2. Bullies—Fiction. 3. Prejudices—Fiction. 4. Obesity—Fiction.
5. Family problems—Fiction. 6. Schools—Fiction.] I. Title.
PZ7.M1905 Lar 2006   [Fic]—dc22   2005032757

Published in the United States by Dutton Children's Books,
a division of Penguin Young Readers Group
345 Hudson Street, New York, New York 10014
www.penguin.com/youngreaders

Designed by Beth Herzog

Printed in USA   First Edition
3 5 7 9 10 8 6 4 2

To Joe, my husband, my best friend, my first reader

ACKNOWLEDGMENT

I would like to thank my amazing editor, Maureen Sullivan, for sharing my vision and enthusiasm for this book from the very start. Working with you has been a dream come true.

Table of Contents

Larger-Than-Life
LARA

1

Character

This isn't about me. This story, I mean. So already you got a reason to hang it up. At least that's what Mrs. Smith, our English teacher says. She teaches fourth graders in Paris, Missouri. But I think she'd about a hundred million times rather be in Paris, France, writing her own stories, instead of teaching us how to write stories.

So anyways, she says you got to start with a character when you start your story. And since I'm the first "character" you hear from in my story, that should mean it's about me. Laney Grafton, age ten, or nearly so, small for her age, but tough as a horseshoe, thanks to three big brothers and one bathroom. Stringy, brownish hair and brown eyes. Not much to look at, but couldn't make a living scaring crows neither.

But it's not. About me. Because once you get you a character for your story, Mrs. Smith says you give the character a problem. And the whole rest of the story's about that problem getting bigger and bigger, and the character getting to be a better and better person, and then the character solves the problem. And that's it. The end.

Only it's not me what's got the problem. And I'm not a better person than I was three months ago when all this stuff happened—just ask my dad or any of my three stupid brothers, if you don't believe me. So, like I said, this story's not about me. And Mrs. Smith, if you're out there reading it, well, I'm just sorry about that. But that's the way it is. Sometimes stories don't work out like they're supposed to.

2

The Beginning

The first thing that happened was that everybody in the whole fourth-grade class, and that includes Mrs. Smith, stopped talking. She was right in the middle of telling us about William Shakespeare, who invented plays in England. Plus, she was telling us about a play our whole school was going to put on and how some of us could be in it and others of us would be really important, but not onstage and that shouldn't make us feel bad. And we were all looking at Mrs. Smith because she gets real mad at us when we don't. I was watching the way her eyes changed size when she finished each sentence, getting bigger, like periods stretching into exclamation points.

So anyways, that was the first thing. I heard quiet.

The second thing was the air changed. Now this is where Mrs. Smith and Amanda Catron and Tommy Otto would argue with me. But this is my story, and I say that the air in our classroom changed. It was hot, lemon-drop sweating hot, so as even Maddie Simpson looked like she'd tiptoed through a water sprinkler. And I'm not saying that the air turned to ice or nothing. But I stopped sweating. So there you have it.

There must have been footsteps because nobody, especially a kid who looked like this one, big as a sofa, could just sneak into a room without them. But I didn't hear any footsteps. And my daddy says I can hear a cat whisper. (When he's been drinking, he says the cats in China can hear *me*, which is his way of saying shut up, and he has other ways of saying shut up, but you can't write them into a story. Mrs. Smith would call this part a digression. So I'm thinking I can get away with it because it's all inside these parentheses.)

Before I saw who had come into our room and changed the air, I saw Joey Gilbert see her. Joey looked like he'd just spotted a ghost, or maybe his mother coming to get him after the principal's kicked him out of school for a week for punching a littler kid. Then I saw Marissa see her. Marissa is so shy, you almost never see her face. But at that minute, her face was on full view, and it was nearly all eyes and mouth dropped open.

Then I saw her. I've seen her so much since that very first time that it's honest-to-pete hard to say what I thought she looked like. And this is something I never thought about as a writer of real things you haven't made up. It's not easy to write the truth, even when that's all you set out to do.

I guess I remember thinking that this was the biggest girl I'd ever seen. Right away I wondered if she was stuck in the doorway, because she was still standing there, filling up the whole space, it seemed to me, with no light from the hallway showing behind her. I figured she was about the most mountainlike human being I'd ever seen, or maybe hill-like, with ridges and rolling fields. And maybe I thought that because she was wearing a green dress, so it looked even more like hills, how the green swelled around her middle and arms. And I'm sure about the green dress because it's what she always wore to school.

"Whoa!" Eric Radabaugh was the first one to start up talking, of course. And Wayne wasn't far behind.

"Man, is the circus in town?" Wayne whispered. Only his whisper is about a hundred times louder than a normal person's regular voice.

I risked looking at the stranger's face to see how she took it. But her round cheeks didn't even twitch, and those pale blue eyes stayed twinkling, like they were smiling, even though her mouth wasn't. So I figured she hadn't heard Eric and Wayne because when they call me "freak girl" or "Toughie" (and I guarantee they don't mean it in a good way), or "hillbilly," there's no way I can pretend I didn't hear.

"Can I help you?" Mrs. Smith asked, clearing her throat, like being hoarse was why she didn't say something before Eric and Wayne got to.

"I'm Lara." The girl's mouth joined her eyes in that smile. She glanced around the room, like she was giving each of us a little piece of her smile.

I looked down at my fingernails when I could tell that smile was getting to my row. Dirt was packed under the nails that weren't bit down to the finger. So I tried picking the dirt out. I don't go around dirty. Really I don't. But nails and ears, those are parts you forget about. At least I do. There's this picture of my mama in the bottom drawer of my daddy's dresser, underneath the magazines he doesn't want my brothers to look at.

And it doesn't take but one look at that picture to know my mama never ever forgot about dirt under her fingernails.

"I'm sorry," Mrs. Smith said. "Laura . . . ?"

"Lara," the girl said, not like she was mad or anything. "L-A-R-A."

"I see." But you could tell our teacher did not see. "Were you looking for someone?"

L-A-R-A's smile got big enough to show us her tiny, white teeth. One of the front ones was missing, and that made her look stranger than fiction. She stayed there, standing in the exact center of the room.

Sometimes Mrs. Smith makes us do these exercises on describing characters when we write stories in class. Characterization, she calls it. She passes out papers that look like this:

_____ *is the kind of person who* _____
_____ *is the kind of person who* _____
_____ *is the kind of person who* _____
_____ *is the kind of person who* _____

Then we fill in the blanks for all the characters in our stories. Well, my mind was filling in all the blanks like this:

Lara *is the kind of person who* <u>changes the air in a</u> <u>classroom.</u>

Lara *is the kind of person who* <u>would be the only</u> <u>one left in Kansas if a tornado blew everybody</u> <u>else to Oz.</u> (Mrs. Smith wouldn't like this one, though, because it's too long.)

Lara *is the kind of person* <u>nobody ever sees, even</u> <u>though she's the biggest thing in the room.</u>

Lara *is the kind of person who* <u>makes *you* feel al-</u> <u>most normal.</u>

Lara *is the kind of person* <u>you never forget.</u>

3

A Frozen Moment

All of this happened in just a couple of seconds, I guess, but it felt like it was a frozen piece of time. Mrs. Smith told us about "frozen moments." Sometimes whole countries and even the whole world has stuff happen that people will remember for the rest of their lives. Like Mrs. Smith said she knows people who were alive when President John F. Kennedy got shot and killed dead. And every single one of them can tell you where they were and what they were wearing and who else and what else was in the room with them when that president got shot and killed.

And I believe her because I can tell you exactly where I was on the day of 9/11, when the planes flew into the World Trade Center. I was home sick from school, only I was faking sick. And I was all by myself, watching TV. Only I'm not supposed to let on I was by myself because the social worker will get after my daddy again. I was wearing the pajamas I hate because they have kites on them and I've never ever had a kite, even though I would really like one.

The room smelled like tobacco and bananas. There was a buzzing from the TV because Daddy hooked it up himself to cable so we didn't have to pay, and sometimes it looked like it was snowing, even on shows like *Jungle Animal Planet*. Then I was changing channels and saw a plane stuck in a skyscraper, with smoke and fire and people screaming. So I thought it was a movie and I'd watch it. Only . . . well, you know the rest. That was a really long digression, and I'm sorry I didn't put it in parentheses.

But the stuff about frozen moments is important because if you land into one, then you got some good material for your story. Because you can call it up in your head again and have everything you need right there. It doesn't go away on you, like other memories. It's frozen. And this can be a good thing or a bad thing.

So back to L-A-R-A, frozen there in the doorway. I remember smelling something that made me think of the school halls on Mondays or my sort-of friend Theresa's house when her mother was cleaning, which was about every single time I've been over there. I remember the backs of kids' heads, all about the same size, most of them brown, with a few blonds mixed in. And Amanda, who has red hair.

Somebody dropped a book, and we all jumped like we'd been shot.

Lara's hair looked thin and fine, the color of chicken gravy.

"Well . . . Lara," Mrs. Smith said, "I'm sorry. Could I help you find something?"

"No thank you," she said, as if our teacher had just offered her a chocolate bar, but she'd already eaten a dozen of them. She said every single consonant and vowel in her words. It made me think of the way our principal talks when she's speaking into the microphone for assemblies. "I've found what I was looking for, I believe," Lara continued. "This is my classroom. I am a new student."

"Oh, my goodness! I'm so sorry!" Mrs. Smith was sorry again and had said so two times in the space of fifteen seconds. I hadn't heard her sorry in the two weeks since school had started. She hurried down the aisle to the new girl. "I thought you'd be here last week. Then I guess I forgot. Lara Phelps, isn't it?"

Lara nodded.

Mrs. Smith walked up to her and stood in front of her, but didn't seem to know whether to shake her hand or take her arm. So she didn't do either one and ended up holding her own arms.

It surprised me to see Mrs. Smith was a head taller than the new girl because I would have guessed the other way around. But it must have been because overall, Lara was bigger. Like a whole lot bigger. And Mrs. Smith is no skinny model herself. I don't know much about weight because Matt, my middle big brother, broke our scale by throwing it at Robert, my biggest big brother, when Robert took too long in the bathroom one day. But if I were guessing, and if Mrs. Smith weighed a hundred pounds, then I'd guess Lara weighed three hundred.

"Well," Mrs. Smith said, like she was superexcited to have a three-hundred-pound student added to the class, "let's find you a seat, shall we?"

I knew because it was my week to do head count that we had twenty-one kids in our class. And we had twenty-two desks. So you'd think that would be okay.

Only there was no way that three hundred pounds of student was going to fit in that desk, which was really just a chair with a desk arm over it, and the arm opens up so you can shove your stuff inside it.

Mrs. Smith turned to the empty chair, which just happened to be next to mine. She stared at it, like she hadn't ever seen such a chair before, like she was wondering how the thing got into her room.

"She'll break it into a hundred million pieces!" Joey cried.

"Joey!" Mrs. Smith snapped. "Keep your mouth closed." She turned back to Lara then. "Tell you what," she said. "I'm going to work on getting you another . . . a chair . . . a desk." She glanced at her watch. "It's just about recess time. Why don't we all go out to recess?"

I think Theresa said something like, "Yes!" And I think Wayne yelled, "Cool! Recess! First bat!"

But the frozen moment was all over by then, so I can't be sure about that part because the words aren't frozen like the rest of it. And besides, I was busy wondering what a person that big could do with recess.

4
Villain

It was at that first recess that Joey Gilbert earned this part in the story. And that is, the role of the villain. Mrs. Smith calls it other things, too. Like antihero, which means against the hero, and so that name fits, too, because Joey Gilbert was against Lara Phelps from the very beginning. In old movies, there's always a villain, especially in Westerns. I know this because my littlest big brother, Luke, would watch cowboys all day Sunday if my daddy didn't kick him off the couch and change the channel to the Rams game. Only in

Westerns, this character would just be known as "the bad guy."

I was keeping my eye on Lara Phelps as we raced out to recess. She didn't actually race. So she was the last one out of the school. I hung back, and I could hear a *swish, swish* when she walked. It was the fat of one leg brushing up against the fat of the other leg. It looked real hard to walk that way, like she had to haul each leg around by her hip, swinging it, so as one foot would move forward.

My daddy says I'm skinny as a willow branch. Robert, my biggest big brother, says I'm so thin I look the same coming as going. Matt, my middle big brother and the meanest of the lot, hardly ever talks to me, except to shout, "Get out of the way, toilet face!" Or other pet names you can't write in books because of censorship and people who'll burn books with dirty words in them, which this one does not have. And even when Joey Gilbert, who is the villain of the story, starts hurling off a list of bad words that would make a sailor sneeze, I won't put those words into the story. Instead, I'll put in other words, but you'll know what I mean. And if that makes part of this story a lie, then it's really just fiction, and that's the way it's got to be. And at least there won't be a good reason for anybody to burn it when it's all done.

Recess isn't as fun as it used to be. Theresa and I used to play baseball with the boys every recess and sometimes after school. And we were as good as all the boys, except for Roger Steeby and maybe Joey Gilbert, on a good day, which he doesn't have many of. I was the best out in the field or on any of the bases because I could run faster than any boy in my class, on account of having been chased by my big brothers, and sometimes even by my daddy if he was drinking. Theresa wasn't so fast. But she's left-handed, and she could get a hit every single time at bat.

Anyway, the stupid boys in my class, led by Joey and Roger, told us at the start-up of fourth grade that we couldn't play with them anymore at recess because it was an all-boys game, which is fine with me, sort of. Although I miss that.

So on Lara Phelps's first day, I wasn't in such a big fat hurry to get to the playground, like I would have been if Joey and Roger hadn't made their boys-only rule. I just sat on a swing and snuck peeks at Lara as she shuffled down the walk. By the time she made it all the way to the playground, the other fourth-grade class got let out, too. They came screaming and yelling down the sidewalk. Until they got to Lara. Then they either ran around her, way around her . . . or they stopped and elbowed each other or put their hands over their mouths, or just yelled back at other kids, stuff like:

"Tony, get a load of this!"

"Megan, look!"

"Jumpin' Jumbo!"

"Truck woman!"

"What—! Oh, man!"

And other things. Some of them you can't put in books.

But she kept on walking, and smiling, sometimes right at the person who said stuff, sometimes just smiling, like to herself. She was breathing heavy by the time she got near the swings. I pretended not to see her, but I could. I could see tiny pearls of sweat on her upper lip.

I kept swinging and dragging one foot so it made me go crooked. Theresa, she was on the other swing next to me, asked, "Laney, is she coming our way? You don't think she's going to try to swing, do you?"

I didn't answer her. But I'd been wondering the same thing, because the swings were just a piece of canvas or something, like a strap the size of a normal person's rear end. And I was pretty sure Lara's rear end wouldn't fit. And if it did fit, the whole swing would break and maybe the whole entire swing set. And if the swing didn't break, how would we ever get her out of there?

But I still wasn't looking.

Then I saw a ball zip past me.

"Fatty! Catch!" Joey Gilbert had fired one at her.

I heard the *thud* of the ball as it hit Lara's upper arm. So I looked. The white ball seemed to be swallowed up into her flesh for a second. It disappeared, then plopped out to the ground. I knew it had to hurt like Harry. But she didn't say nothing, and I swear on my middle big brother's life that her smile didn't so much as twitch. She leaned over—which sent the kids behind her into fits of laughing—and picked up the ball. Then she tossed it back to Joey. The ball made a little arc, like a rainbow, and only got halfway to where Joey was standing.

Joey had to walk up close to her to get his ball. "Hey, fat girl!" he shouted, although he was so close he wouldn't have had to shout. "What's your name?"

"Lara," she answered, as if Joey wasn't a wing nut for not knowing her name, even though the teacher had said it a bunch of times. And as if Joey hadn't just whipped a ball right into her arm. "What's yours?"

I stared hard at them then, because I knew her asking his name would throw Joey off his guard. He wasn't asking her name in the "and what's *your* name?" kind of niceness, like he would have done if Lara had looked like Maddie Simpson.

"Huh?" Joey said. "What—I'm not—"

"Go on, Joey!" Wayne hollered. He was standing off with Roger and Eric, huddled together and watching their fearless leader.

Joey waved them off with his glove. Then he did this kind of snorting laugh and eyed Lara up and down, shaking his head all the while, like he just couldn't believe his own eyes. "I just come over here to warn you to stay off the swings and everything else out here because you'll just break everything with your big fat body."

This brought wild laughter from Joey's all-boy cheering section.

Ashley and Maddie and their crowd came trotting up, too, and formed a line behind Joey. They giggled like they were in first grade, instead of fourth.

Theresa laughed. She's kind of chubby, and I got the feeling she wasn't entirely against the idea of having somebody in class who made her look skinny.

I got to admit that I laughed, too. But it wasn't a real laugh, and I guess that makes it worse.

Joey, you could tell, was loving the audience. He glanced from the guys to the girls, then back to Lara. "Man, you're the biggest darn kid I ever did see! Lara, huh? Larger than life."

Lara probably didn't get it, but it came from a story Mrs. Smith read to us the first week of school. She'd said the characters in that story were larger than life.

"Hey!" Joey exclaimed, looking like a lightbulb just went off inside his head and was burning his pea brain. "That's a great name for you—Larger-than-life Lara!"

5

Setting

I know good and well that if Mrs. Smith is reading this, she's real disappointed about me not having any setting to speak of and we're already to chapter five. But I don't think it's all my fault. I mean, school classrooms are about the most boring places you can write about. What would I say so as I could have some setting for the story? Four walls, two with blackboards on them, only they're really white boards, and instead of chalk, big markers sit on little silver ledges? Big interesting set. All classrooms look alike. That's how come you can get so mixed up when you're a really little kid and you keep going into the wrong classroom because they all look alike.

Or I could say that the floor is blondish, skinny boards. And the chairs and desk arms are all brown. And now would be the first time I could describe how our room looked a little different from the other rooms in Paris Elementary because Mrs. Smith went and got a special-made desk for Lara. That twenty-second desk was really a big teacher's chair and a folding table that fit in front of it.

So that's a little interesting, but there's not much more setting at school, if you ask me. And not too much more happened the rest of Lara Phelps's first day either because by the time we got back from afternoon recess, there wasn't enough school left for anything interesting to happen.

When school got let out, I watched Lara waddle to an old blue minivan. She climbed up into the back of that van, even though that was no easy thing to do, and there wasn't no other person in that van except for a regular-size man driving. And it turned out that was her daddy, and he picked her up every single day after school.

I bounced out of there fast after that and headed home. I walked because I hate the school bus. There's a lot of setting on that bus, but none of it's good. It takes me twenty minutes to walk home, but it's better than two minutes on the bus with the likes of Joey Gilbert and three fifth-grade boys who think they own the bus.

The sun was still full-strength hot, with not so much as a cloud hanging in the sky. Some of the leaves on top of maple trees were starting to burn brown.

After I turned off School Street, which is the real live name for it, I lost the sidewalk and took to the left side of the gravel road leading out of town. Nearly every step stirred up grasshoppers. That's how dry it had been all summer. Locusts buzzed in bushes as I walked past the Methodist church. Some people call it singing, what those crickets and locusts do, and I suppose that would make for a prettier piece of setting all right, but it still sounds like buzzing to me.

A few kids walked as far as Orange Street ahead of me. But I was the only one kept going past the old railroad tracks, on beyond the cemetery, and around the fork to our place.

There's a lot of setting at my house.

My house is a peeling white box made of boards, with two windows in front. The funny thing is that the windows are different sizes. One's tall and thin, a rectangle. The other's short and fat, a square. So when you look head-on at our house, it seems like the house is winking at you. There's a front porch that needs a rail and maybe new steps. But we don't go in the front anyway. Two rusted-out cars propped up on gray blocks sprawl out over the weedy lawn. There's a lilac bush out back that grew all by itself, but it didn't have any flowers on it.

Nobody was home when I walked in through the back door, which wasn't locked, like it never is. Daddy says anybody fool enough to steal from a Grafton ought to have his head examined. My brothers are only in seventh, eighth, and ninth grade, but they've already got themselves a reputation. So does my daddy. He works at the parts factory and has won more than his share of fights. Sometimes I hear about them at school. I've never seen the inside of the parts factory, but I'd bet my middle big brother's eyes that there's a whole lot of setting in there.

I opened the fridge because I was real hungry. But I already knew everything that was in there because I do all the grocery shopping. Chocolate pudding in plastic cups. An opened can of spaghetti, apples, some of them mushy. Hot dogs and baloney were in the meat drawer.

I shut the fridge and just got peanut butter out of the jelly cupboard and ate a couple of spoonfuls of that.

There were two little boxes of macaroni-and-cheese mix, which I thought about making for supper. That's one thing I don't have to do—cook for everybody. Daddy says we're all big enough to fend for ourselves, and that's what we do. I don't see any reason why I should cook for my brothers, just because I'm the girl. And I'm not making their beds either. They can just go and get themselves a maid, if that's what they want. That's what I tell them. When I told Matt this, he threw his pillow at me and hit me in the head with it, but it didn't hurt. Then he threw his boot at me, but I ducked and it missed. And it *would* have hurt if it hit.

But tonight, I wanted to cook up the macaroni for Daddy and me because I had to ask him something that I thought he might be more likely to say yes to if he had a nice, hot plate of macaroni and cheese in front of him. The thing I had to ask him about was Mrs. Smith's play. I wanted to try out to be in it.

Joey Gilbert says plays are stupid. I never let on in school, but I love those plays. I even checked out a written-down play by that Shakespeare guy. I had to take it back to the library the next day because the

English they talked back then wasn't easy to understand like our English. But the stuff I could understand was really good and some of it even rhymed, which is not easy to do in case you never tried it.

I might be an actress when I get out of school. I know this sounds like something a little kid would say. Then all the grown-ups would say back, "How cute," or, "Isn't that sweet?" Except for if I said this to my daddy, he would probably say I should stop being a dumbhead and that people like us don't make a living like that. This was why I knew I needed the macaroni.

Mrs. Smith's play was called *Fair Day*, and there were lots of girl parts. Some of the characters in that play come and visit the fair. And other of the characters have animals they show at the fair. Mrs. Smith said we couldn't have real animals. But it would still be a really good play. Joey Gilbert said *Fair Day* sounded like the dumbest play he'd ever heard of.

This would be my first official play, but I acted all the time. Like when Daddy asked me, "How's school?" I'd say, "Fine," and he believed me. And when Mrs. Smith or somebody asked, "How are things at home?" and I'd say, "Just fine," they'd believe me, too. So I figured I was a pretty good actress and always had been.

I pulled out the macaroni box and hid it behind the cereal in the cupboard over the sink.

The door slammed. I recognized the footsteps of my littlest big brother, Luke. "Hey! I'm starving!" he screamed from the back porch. He stomped into the kitchen and threw his backpack on the floor. Luke never says "hi" or "how are you?" like a normal person. "What's there to eat?"

"Pepperoni pizza, bacon cheeseburgers, chocolate milk shakes, and homemade brownies," I answered.

"Shut up, Laney," he said.

I almost forgot to say that our kitchen has an old stove on one wall. It's white, but it has a chip out of it up front, and there's a Band-Aid over that chip, and it's been there for as long as I can remember. Only two of the four black burners work, but we don't care. Under one small, smudged window is a sink with a dripping, snake-necked faucet. There's also an orangish brown refrigerator, which I told you what it had in it. And a wooden table with four chairs that don't match each other. If we ever did want to eat together, we'd have to pull in a chair from the living room. The floor is gray linoleum with red and white specks in it, which comes in handy because when there's food or dirt on the floor, it pretty much just looks like the specks in the linoleum.

Whoever had the house before we did painted all the rooms lime green and we figure they must have gotten that paint at a supersale, and no wonder it was on supersale because who wants lime green. But we got used to it.

Luke grabbed two puddings from the fridge and took them to the silverware drawer for a spoon.

Then the next person who stormed in hungry was Robert. Robert's in high school, ninth grade, and he doesn't look much like Luke or Matt. People say Robert got the good looks in the family. He's tall and has blond hair, instead of brown like the rest of us. But he's got Daddy's squinty, hard eyes. I don't know who I look like, but I hope I got some of my mama in me. It's hard to tell with only the one picture of her, and that's hid under magazines in a bottom drawer. But she's not dead. Just run away. So someday I'll see her and can tell if we look alike or not.

Robert went straight to the jelly cupboard instead of the fridge. He also got the brains in the family. I was glad I'd seen to the macaroni and hidden it already. "Didn't you get anything good to eat, Laney?" he growled.

Luke spoke up before I could. "Pepperoni pizza, bacon cheeseburgers, brownies—"

Robert smacked him on the back of his head. "Shut up, Luke. You're not funny."

I kept my mouth shut and went to the living room.

I about had a cow when I saw Matt on the couch. The couch is almost the same green as the paint on the walls, and this is a coincidence. Matt was stretched out on the couch, his dirty legs and bare feet hanging over one arm. There were bowls and newspaper and wrappers on the carpet. Our rug is called "shag," and that's a good name for it because it looks like it belongs on the back of a brown shaggy dog. It smells kind of doggy, too. I never sit on the floor in the living room. Plus if I do, my legs itch.

From the look of things, Matt had been home a long time. I guess I was standing in front of the TV because he shouted, "Get out of the way, zit head!" He pointed the remote at me, and the TV turned on, and I made sure I got out of the way.

I figured Matt hadn't bothered to go to school at all. But I wasn't about to say so. Like I said, Matt is the meanest of my big brothers.

Robert came in. "What are you doing home, Matt? You ditch again?"

"You're not my mother!" Matt said. He pointed the remote again, and the volume went up so loud he probably couldn't hear what Robert said next.

Which is a good thing because if I wrote it in this story, this book could get burned.

The last place for setting was my room, which is where I went so I didn't have to listen to Matt and Robert yelling at each other.

Upstairs should be an attic, but we split it into two rooms with a blanket down the middle. Daddy has one room, and I have the other. The roof slants, so there are places you can't stand up without bumping your head, especially Daddy, because he's six feet tall.

The walls are green, like downstairs. Mrs. Smith says that a setting, like a character's room, should tell you something about your character. I don't see how mine tells much about me. But here goes.

My bed is a mattress on the floor against one wall, with a little window above it. Three things are stuck on my walls. 1) A shelf made of wood, stained and varnished. My dad made it himself and put it up on my wall right where I said I wanted it. And it's the nicest thing he ever gave me. I keep books on it. Sometimes the library has old books for quarters. And our school librarian gives me books she'd have to throw away otherwise. I have *The Secret Garden*, which is so old the covers aren't stuck to the pages. And *Because of Winn-Dixie*, which is a book we read last year and all got us a copy. Some kids didn't even want theirs, so I have three of them. I've got a couple of animal books, with rabbits as characters or mice. Mrs. Smith makes us write about people instead of animals, and she would be happy to know that there aren't any animals in this book so far, unless you count locusts and crickets and grasshoppers. But if I do write a story about animals, it will probably be about turkeys, and they won't get killed for Thanksgiving. Because I think turkeys have a pretty hard life.

2) The second thing on my wall is a tennis shoe. I'm probably the only fourth grader in all of Missouri who has a tennis shoe glued to her lime green wall. But last year I beat Roger Steeby and Joey Gilbert and every other boy in both third grades in a race our school had for Fitness Week. And it was official. Our teacher started the race by blowing his whistle, and everybody watched it. So when my shoes got too small, which they almost were before the race even, and my toes stuck through, then I glued one shoe to my wall so I wouldn't never forget what that felt like to have people cheering for me.

3) The third thing on my wall is a poster Ms. Gib-

son, our school librarian, gave me when she fixed up her library with all new stuff. The poster is a picture of a theater. Not the movie kind of theater. The Globe Theatre. It's where Shakespeare acted out his fancy plays. I really like that poster a lot.

And looking at it reminded me about the play I wanted to be in and how I would have to get my daddy's permission to even try out because if I did win a part, I'd have to stay after school and practice. And getting my daddy to say okay to that one was going to take a lot more than macaroni and cheese.

6

Dialogue

"Dialogue" is the conversation between two or more people in a book or a play. That's what Mrs. Smith taught us. It's really just talk. She said readers like lots of it. I looked back through the first five chapters of my book, and I'm pretty sure that so far I don't have enough dialogue. So I'm going to try to make up for it now.

But there are some hard things about dialogue. Like for instance, one thing is you have to talk to people. I don't do this a whole lot. Robert and Matt and Luke don't like to talk to me, and I don't like to talk to them.

At school, Theresa and I talk some, especially when her best friend, Amanda, isn't speaking to her or is absent. Although if we do this in class, Mrs. Smith yells at us. Besides which, Theresa and Amanda's biggest problems are too little, like whether they should get their hair cut or not. And my biggest problems are too big to talk about, so that's the first hard thing.

The next hard thing about dialogue is that it's hard to get all the words right. This doesn't matter if you're just making stuff up. But my book isn't making stuff up. And I'm trying not to put words into people's mouths if the words didn't actually come out of their mouths. Still, I got to say straight out that maybe I forgot some of the dialogue and even that maybe I forgot some of it on purpose.

When I came down from my bedroom, Matt was on the phone. Robert was sitting on the couch with Matt, eating a hot dog and watching the sports part of the news. Luke was sitting on the floor, throwing things out of his backpack, like he was searching for something. There was no dialogue when I came down, if you don't count the sports men talking to themselves on the TV.

Then Matt slammed down the phone and glared at me. "Hey, why didn't you tell me you had an elephant girl at your school?"

"What's an elephant girl?" Luke asked.

"Shut up!" Matt answered.

"There's no such thing as an elephant girl," Robert said.

I didn't say anything yet.

"Travis said his brother's class got a new girl who's big as an elephant," Matt explained. "Roger and Laney are in the same class." He turned back to me. "So?"

Luke quit searching through his bag and came closer to join in the dialogue. "No lie, Laney? Does she look like an elephant?"

I shrugged. (This is not exactly dialogue. Mrs. Smith says it's a gesture.)

"Is she just normal fat, like Theresa?" Robert asked.

I shook my head. Another gesture.

"So?" Matt demanded. "Is she really as fat as Travis says, or is his brother a liar?"

"Yes and yes. Roger is a liar. And I'll bet she weighs three hundred pounds," I said, walking in front of the TV on purpose. It almost never happened that even one of my brothers made dialogue with me, so this was really something that all three of them wanted to ask me questions.

Robert made a sound that might have been a guffaw.

I've seen this word written in stories when it seemed like the characters were laughing. But I could be wrong about Robert's noise because I don't know if I've ever heard a real guffaw. "Is there room for this new fat kid in a regular classroom?" he asked.

Before I could answer, Matt jumped off the couch and shoved me aside from the TV. Then he asked, "Did you talk to her, Laney?"

"What's she like?" Luke asked.

I was getting a not-so-good feeling, like they were tired of me not having the answers they wanted. And that meant trouble. For me.

"What's with you, Laney?" Matt snarled. (I'm not sure you can use *snarl* in dialogue. But Matt made me think of the Baileys' pit bull that's always about an inch away from biting a person. So *snarl* works for me.) "What's her name? Who is she? Didn't you even try to find out?"

"Her name is Lara. Larger-than-life Lara. And she's my new best friend," I said, which was an out-and-out lie because I hadn't said so much as one word to her. Plus, I had no plans to. "And," I went on, "she said to tell you that if you give me trouble, she'll come over here and sit on you."

. . .

That ended that dialogue, and I went to the kitchen. I figured that all three boys had already stuffed their faces, so it was safe to get out the macaroni mix.

The macaroni had been sitting on the stove in the pan for so long that it had all mushed together, when I heard Daddy's truck. I knew as soon as I heard it scrape up the gravel drive that his and my dialogue was going to be tougher than I thought. He was driving too fast, and he had to slam on the brakes to miss hitting the shed. If the car had been dialoguing with the driveway, it would have looked like this:

"ERRRRK!" screamed the brakes.

"Crunch, crush!" growled the gravel.

I stirred the mushy macaroni and worried about how it might not be so much help at persuading Daddy to let me try out for the play. I already had the table set with two places, which had caused some not-so-nice dialogue from Robert and Matt, who right away said they knew I was up to something. Or did I invite my new girlfriend over for dinner?

"Hey, Daddy!" I called as he stumbled into the kitchen. "I made you dinner."

"Hey, Laney," he said. He came over and sniffed the macaroni in the pan. "I ain't had nothing to eat. Them stooges down at the factory cut lunch break a good five minutes. One of these days, I'm going out for lunch and not going back at all. I swear."

My daddy has worked at the parts factory for twelve years. Sometimes he comes home smelling like oil from a car. Other times, of which tonight was one, he smells like beer. I'm not sure which smell I hate worse.

We sat at the table and started in on our macaroni. I was real grateful that all three boys had run out of the house after Matt got another phone call. I didn't know where they were, and Daddy didn't ask after them.

We ate without any dialogue for a while. I knew I had to start it.

"Guess what," I said.

He didn't. He got up and took a beer out of the fridge, popped the top, and sat back down.

"We got a new girl in class today."

He took a long swig from the can. "Hmmm."

"She's really big. Bigger than Mr. Rafer." Mr. Rafer was one of Daddy's bosses.

"That son of a sodbuster. He thinks he can make us do overtime without paying for it." He took another swig. "Well, that not-nice man has another think coming."

(This was not his real dialogue. But I figure you know that. And you know why.)

"The new girl's name's Lara, and we had to get her a table for her desk," I continued, trying to get him off Mr. Rafer because that had been a mistake to bring up.

"You know what, Laney?" He narrowed his tiny eyes at me, like he was going to tell me something that was going to change my life forever. "Don't you never settle. You hear?" He downed his beer. So far he hadn't eaten more than two bites of the macaroni. Me neither. But he got up and got himself another can of beer.

I figured I better get the show on the road because he was either going to end up mad and shouting, or he was going to fall asleep right over his bowl of macaroni.

"Daddy?"

"Hmmm."

"I agree with you about not settling."

"Uh-huh."

"So I've got something to ask you. Because I don't want to settle, like you said not to."

"Hmm?"

"At school, Mrs. Smith says we're going to put on a play. And the play is by Samuel Green, and it's called *Fair Day*. And you got to memorize lines and even sing a song. And to do that, you got to practice. The practices are after school sometimes, so that means not getting home right after."

"I wanted to be in a play once."

"Well, so, you know what I mean!"

"Stupid sons of not-nice fathers wouldn't let me. Never did get to."

"So I need your permission to even just try out for it."

"I wasn't good enough for them. Graftons weren't to amount to nothing."

"Is it okay? Can I tell Mrs. Smith it's okay?"

"Huh?"

"Please say yes, Daddy."

"Yes? Sure. Whatever my baby wants. I'm going to watch the game." He got up, took another beer from the fridge, and left.

I heard the TV come on.

In my head, I replayed our dialogue. I'd asked him straight up about being in the play. And he'd said yes. So that was that.

I knew if he hadn't been drinking, he probably wouldn't have said yes. He counts on me to keep the boys from killing each other when he's not home. And he doesn't like me to go to other people's houses after school, not that anybody 'sides Theresa ever asks me to.

I was pretty sure he wasn't going to remember about the *Fair Day* play in the morning, or about him saying yes. But he said it. And that was enough for me to do the trying out.

Besides, I dialogued to myself, *I probably won't get a part in the play anyhow. Graftons don't get parts in plays.*

7

Opposition

Mrs. Smith says the middle of a story can be the most boringest part. And I think she's right. Because that's where sometimes some kids fall asleep when we have reading time. So she says the middle part is where you have to get you some opposition, which means things or people that are against your character. Which was not a problem in this book because Larger-than-life Lara had so much opposition it can't all fit in here, or the story would be so long that nobody, not even Mrs. Smith, would read every word of it.

Mrs. Smith said that some famous writer who I can't think of the name of right now said, "It's a good book, but the covers are too far apart." Get it? Like the middle part of the book was way too big and fat. I don't want that to happen to me. And another writer I can't remember said, "Inside every big, fat book is a skinny book waiting to come out." And I'm not so sure what that one means, but it made Mrs. Smith laugh, and it's true because a famous writer said so.

So what you do, then, about opposition, is you pick the biggest or most interesting ones. And that's what I'm doing.

I got to school Tuesday after Joey and before Lara. So I, along with most of the kids in my class, saw Joey Gilbert put a folded piece of paper on Lara's larger-than-life desk. Doing this made Maddie and Sara and Amber giggle, so I figured they knew more about this note than I did, which didn't surprise me none. Somebody would have had to help Joey spell the words, for one thing. He was the worst speller in the whole class, if you didn't count Eric.

Joey shot me this look that Matt, my meanest big brother, gives me when he thinks I might tell on him. Only Joey's got a ways to go with that look. He should have known I never tell on anybody. I stay out of trouble that's not mine.

Lara was the last one to come in the classroom, and I was thinking that if I was her, I'd be the first one so as I wouldn't have to walk down the side of the class (she didn't fit between desk aisles) and have everybody staring at me. But she smiled, like she was so glad to be back and was having good memories of her first day at Paris Elementary.

"Now, then," Mrs. Smith began, "for our reading time today, we're going to start reading through *Fair Day*. It's a fine little play, written by a man who used to farm in this community."

I watched out of the corner of my eye as Lara grunted into her desk.

"We should finish reading the play tomorrow. If you're trying out for a part, I'll be passing out copies of tryout portions of the script tomorrow. But don't forget that everyone will have a part in our production."

She went into her routine about how lighting and making the background and decorating the stage were all just as good as being a star on the stage. I missed a lot of the speech because I was watching Lara unfold her note.

"Excuse me, class?" This was Mrs. Smith's way of saying "Shut up!" although sometimes she just said that. "Would someone care to tell me what's so interesting that you can't pay attention to me?"

I glanced around the room. Kids were creeping out of their seats and stretching to see what Lara was going to do about Joey's note.

"You know how I feel about passing notes in class," Mrs. Smith said, stretching out her arm to Lara.

We did know. If Mrs. Smith caught you passing notes, she collected them and read them all in front of God and everybody, even when it was notes between Maddie and Tommy, or some other boy, and they were so mushy that we all said things like, "Yuck!," "Gross!," "Give me a break!"

Since I sat right next to Lara, I had already got me a good look at Joey Gilbert's note. And I was pretty sure Mrs. Smith wouldn't read it out loud. I can't remember every single word of that note, and I can't guarantee I got the words in the right order. But it went something like this:

To Larger-than-life Lara,
You should be the PIG in our play about Fare Day.

Only pigs aren't as fat as you are and they're a heck of a lot prettier, too. Why don't you go back to the pigpen where you belong?

Joey

I don't know why Joey would have signed the note. He's stupid, but not that stupid. I thought maybe who-ever did the spelling for Joey made sure to sign Joey's name so as the speller wouldn't get in trouble.

Lara still hadn't handed over the note to Mrs. Smith, whose arm was still reaching for it. Instead, Lara folded the note. Then she folded it again.

If I didn't think Mrs. Smith would get after me for using a cliché, I would say that in our classroom, you could have heard a pin drop. That's how quiet it got. Clichés are sayings that get too much use and people get sick and tired of them. That's what our teacher says, and she doesn't like them one bit.

When the note was folded as small as it could get, Lara smiled up at Mrs. Smith. Mrs. Smith put down her arm. Her forehead wrinkled up like an even older per-son's, and her head tilted to one side because you could tell she just didn't get what was going on. Then Lara asked, "Mrs. Smith, do you mind if I keep my note?"

"Lara, you don't have to take this," Mrs. Smith began. She turned to Joey Gilbert, who scurried back into his chair. "Joey, I've seen enough to know this note is your doing. This is inexcusable. You and I have to have a little talk with the principal and—"

"Mrs. Smith?" Lara interrupted, so calm and peaceful that Mrs. Smith stopped talking, and her wrinkles went back to the normal ones. "Could I just say something to Joey, instead of you and the principal doing it?"

"What?" asked our teacher.

Lara didn't repeat it. She just kept smiling.

Finally, Mrs. Smith's head nodded yes.

Lara got herself up out of her desk, which I'm telling you, was no small thing to do. Then she turned to the back of the room and smiled directly at Joey Gilbert.

If you thought it was quiet in our room before, when you could have heard a pin drop, you should have heard it now. You could have heard a feather drop.

In my head, I tried to imagine what I would have said, if I'd been Larger-than-life Lara and gotten me a mean note that called me a pig. And first off, I figured that I would have let Mrs. Smith and Principal Russell have at Joey. Then I would have taken him on at recess. I know this to be true because it's already happened to me two times. But he didn't call me a pig—just Hillbilly Jill and stuff like that.

But not Lara. That smile never left her face the whole time. And here's what Lara said.

> "Hey, Joey Gilbert, thanks for the note.
> In a class-clown election, you'd get my vote.
> I watched you pitch, and I think you're great.
> But you'll get more power if your arm is straight."

Then Larger-than-life Lara sat down.

Nobody, not even Mrs. Smith, said nothing while Lara lowered herself back into her chair and scooched her body the rest of the way into it and pulled her folding-table desk as close as it could get to her larger-than-life stomach.

Mrs. Smith started to say something, like, "Well, Lara, that was . . ." then changed her mind and started over with, "Joey, you . . . I never want you . . . again." But she gave up trying to solve the opposition in another way from what Lara had done, and she went back to talking about the play.

A normal person who just got out of having to go to the principal's office for the hundred millionth time, and instead just got himself a pretty good rhyming poem that called him a class clown and great at base-ball, plus gave him good advice on pitching, would have been happy or maybe even grateful. But Joey Gilbert is no normal person. And I had a feeling that he wasn't happy even one little bit about how things turned out.

I didn't turn around to look at Joey until Mrs. Smith started in on reading *Fair Day* to us. But when I did, it didn't take but one look for me to know I was right. Joey Gilbert was not happy. His eyes were slanty. His mouth made a hard line. He was squeezing his pencil so hard it was a miracle it hadn't broke up into pieces.

Mrs. Smith said about opposition that it's boring when the opposition happens and then gets all over with right away. That it's better when the opposition grows and grows and gets bigger and bigger.

That one look at Joey Gilbert made me know for sure that his opposition wasn't the getting-over-fast kind. His was the growing-bigger-and-bigger kind. Like a larger-than-life opposition.

8
Minor Characters

Joey Gilbert is the kind of kid who would never settle for being a minor character in a story. So I will leave him out of this chapter as much as possible. But the truth is that Joey was never very far out of the picture. His opposition just kept growing and growing. Sometimes at recess, where I could swear he started keeping his arm straighter when he pitched, and his pitches started hitting the strike zone every single time. Sometimes in class, where he whispered his meanness, instead of putting it into a note and signing it. But mostly, he was the biggest opposition at lunchtimes.

But he's no minor character, so I'm done talking about him in this chapter.

Maddie Simpson is the kind of person you'd like to look like, if you were to have the secret idea that you wanted to be an actress when you got out of school. She's not too fat or too skinny. Her hair is blond and long and wavy and never looks like she's to the day when it ought to get washed. It doesn't hurt that she wears clothes like the middle-school, and even high-school, girls wear. You hardly ever see her in the same clothes as she's worn before.

Two days before tryouts for *Fair Day* were scheduled to happen, Maddie and her best friend, Sara, surprised the socks off of all of us at first-hour lunch period. (I better say here that Sara is the kind of person who doesn't know if she wants a hot dog or a hamburger, a Pepsi or a Coke, until other people have ordered first.)

They got their trays of cafeteria lunch, like they always did, both of them picking the exact same thing. But instead of going to the head table with the other popular fourth graders, they stood in the middle of the cafeteria and looked all around. Then they weaved through the tables of noisy lunch eaters until they got to Lara's table.

Lara had her own chair in the cafeteria. She'd gotten it after the cafeteria opposition thing that happened with Joey Gilbert. (But I'm not getting into that one here because he's not a minor character.) The janitor set up Lara's lunch chair special, right before first lunch period, and took it away right after. He saw to it that the chair was pushed up to one of the long cafeteria tables, instead of being off by itself. But it ended up off by itself anyway, because nobody—and I mean nobody—ever sat down with Larger-than-life Lara.

I hate lunch. Usually, I sit with Theresa and Amanda, even if they're being best friends and only talking to each other that day. Sometimes a reject boy or two sit at the same table as us, only act like it's a different table, and maybe even a different cafeteria, or even a different school.

Our table was two tables away from the empty table with Lara's chair. Sometimes I'd sneak a peek at her, and she'd look like she was the only one enjoying lunch. Not because she gobbled her lunch or ate more than other kids. She just looked like she enjoyed it because of that smile of hers.

So back to Maddie. She walked right up to Lara. Sara followed her, staying behind, like she was afraid of what Lara might do.

"Are these seats taken?" Maddie asked.

Lara had to know Maddie was up to something because those seats were never taken. "No they're not. Please be seated, Maddie and Sara," Lara answered. Somehow, after a couple of days at our school, and with nobody talking to her, Lara seemed to know every single person's name.

"Thank you," Maddie said fake-sweetly.

Sara still looked scared, but she sat down when Maddie did.

Somebody dropped a tray on the other side of the cafeteria. Silverware clattered on the floor. Somebody busted out laughing. There were kids yelling at each other at the popular tables, where Maddie and Sara ought to have been eating.

There was one table between where I was sitting and Lara's table, but I could hear. Our end of the cafeteria was quieter, for one thing. And for another, not only was Lara's table empty, but the table next to her was empty on that end, like people were afraid fatness was something you could catch if you ate too close to it.

"So how do you like school?" Maddie asked, like they were old friends and she was really interested in something that wasn't about her.

"I love school," Lara said. "Where else can you learn

every day and meet all kinds of new people? What's not to love?"

When Lara said that, you had to believe her. It was something in her eyes and the way the smile didn't go away.

Mrs. Smith taught us that sarcastic is how you're being when you say the opposite from what you really mean. Like when I say to my middle big brother, Matt, "Oh, that's real cute, Matt." Only it isn't. Saying Matt's cute when he isn't is sarcastic. This is not the same thing as lying. When you lie, you don't want the other person to know it's a lie. If you're sarcastic, you want the other person to know you're saying the opposite of what you mean and saying it snotty.

Well, Lara wasn't being sarcastic. In spite of Joey Gilbert's pig note, and in spite of what he did to her later that day in the cafeteria, and in spite of what kids said to her and about her, Lara Phelps liked school.

Lara turned to Sara. "So, Sara, are you trying out for a part in the play, *Fair Day?*"

"Um . . ." Sara glanced at Maddie. "Uh . . . I guess."

Maddie swung around on her. "You didn't tell me you were trying out! I'm supposed to be your best friend. And you didn't say anything to me about it? What part? What part are you trying out for?"

"I think you'd be a great Adeline," Lara said. She took really little bites of food, so it was taking her a long time to finish hot lunch.

"Do you really think I'd be a great Adeline? Really?" Sara asked, her eyes getting big.

"I do," Lara answered. "I heard you sing in music yesterday."

"You heard *me?*" Sara asked. "But you were in the back." Sara and Maddie always sit front-row center in music class. Ms. Brandywine loves them so much she doesn't even yell at them when they giggle and talk all during music period.

Lara nodded. "I still heard you. You're good."

"Wait a minute!" Maddie raised her voice, even though she wouldn't have had to. "*I'm* trying out for Adeline. I told you that."

"I know. I know," Sara said quickly. "And everybody knows you'll get it."

"So." Maddie had control back. "So you can be Adeline's friend. The one who helps her fix her hair when she's going to meet Tom? You know?"

Sara shrugged and nodded at the same time.

And then it seemed to be all settled, when a funny thing happened next. Lara looked up from her tray and stared right at Sara, like Maddie wasn't there sitting between them. She didn't stand up, like she had for Joey in our classroom, but here's what she said:

> "*Sara Rivers, with the silvery voice,*
> *Reach for the stars! It's still your choice.*
> *You can do it, though it's scary.*
> *Fear is so unnecessary.*"

When Lara was done with her rhyming poem, Sara's pink-lipsticked mouth hung open like a snagged fish.

Maddie looked from Lara to Sara like they were in a Ping-Pong match. "I don't get it." All the sweet had gone right out of her voice. "What's wrong with you? Normal people don't just say rhyming things in the middle of the cafeteria. We only came over here because we felt sorry for you. I was going to try to help you by telling you that you should stop eating desserts, for crying out loud. Then maybe you'd start looking like a human, instead of a fat pig."

Sara didn't say anything.

Maddie did. "But since you're the smart one with all the advice . . . here!" She took her own brownie from her tray and banged it down on Lara's tray. Then she grabbed Sara's brownie and shoved it at Lara, too.

"Go ahead!" She stood up and clutched her tray. "Pig out, pig!"

Sara just sat there, staring at her brownie on Lara's tray.

"Sara!" Maddie shouted, from halfway across the cafeteria. Kids stopped horsing around to stare.

Sara hurried up from the table and ran to join Maddie.

There were lots of other minor characters who did things to Lara. And here is one. Eric Radabaugh is the kind of kid who would have been a shark if he'd been an animal. We learned in science that sharks have to keep moving all the time or they'll die dead. And that's Eric. He can't sit still.

Eric went to the pencil sharpener about a hundred times a day. And every time he did, he'd take a left up an aisle, dart another left, squeeze himself between desks, and end up right next to Lara's desk. Then he'd poke her with his pencil, or bump into her, or elbow her. Once, on the way back to his seat, he pretended like he bumped into Lara and bounced off and landed on the floor. Everybody laughed. Which reminds me of Wayne. Wayne Wilson, who, if you can remember back as far as chapter two, you won't be surprised about, was the loudest kid in our class. In fact, the loudest kid in the whole fourth grade and maybe in all of Paris Elementary, and it wouldn't surprise me none if he was the loudest kid in the whole state of Missouri.

Wayne is the kind of kid who's the first to laugh and the last to understand what everybody's laughing at. During that first week of Larger-than-life Lara, Wayne laughed first when the wind caught Lara's skirt after school on Tuesday. And it blew up so as you could see the back of her thigh, which was bigger than a horse's patuney. Wayne laughed the loudest when our teacher had us help her make a list of clichés on the board, and Lara gave her more than the rest of us put together, and they all had to do with fat. Fat as a pig. Big as a house. Big as a barn. The fat of the land. It ain't over until the fat lady sings.

Wayne laughed hard at each and every one. But Mrs. Smith, she said Lara got them all right, and that those sayings really were expressions people use so much that they lose their meaning. Only I wondered about that, about those words losing their meaning.

And last, Wayne was first to laugh when Mrs. Smith asked, "Who's planning on trying out for a part in our play?" and Lara raised her very big arm, and the fat on the bottom part of her arm jiggled.

Finally, in this chapter on minor characters, I got to

add this. Laney Grafton is the kind of person that doesn't do open meanness to a person, but couldn't help being a little glad that the meanness was going to somebody else for a change, because for three whole days nobody called her a name or tripped her at recess.

9

Conflict

Conflict is a whole lot like opposition, and I'm not real sure I know the difference. Opposition is like the other team that's waiting to beat the tar out of you. Conflict is the beating. Or something like that.

Which makes me have to back up to that day when Joey Gilbert gave Lara the pig note, and Lara gave him a poem answer that rhymed. If that note was just opposition, then what happened in the cafeteria after that was conflict.

Mrs. Smith says stories have a beginning, middle, and end. They should get told in a chronological order, which is a fancy way of saying making stuff happen like it did in real life, without jumping back and forth in time like some kind of time traveler. I tried to do that, which is why you can find words like *first* and *next* and *then*, if you go back looking for them in this story.

But I can't figure out how else to tell this one conflict without time traveling backward. So Mrs. Smith, if you're reading this, I just apologize for that.

Tuesday was Lara's first lunch at Paris Elementary because she was too late for it on Monday. When she did that *swish, swish* walk into the cafeteria, people pointed at her (which could also be a cliché to say, but they did it anyway). She waited for her food and got the normal amount as other kids in line. Then she shuffled off with her tray, going to the very back table. You could tell this wasn't her first time in a school cafeteria. She set her tray down on the table, but she didn't have the special chair to sit in. So she was standing up and pushing the little straw that comes with milk into the milk bag. And that's when Joey Gilbert and Wayne and three other characters came along. The three other boy characters are too minor to even have names in this story.

Joey said, "Do you eat standing up?"

Lara smiled at him. "Not usually. I'll sit on the corner here." She lowered herself onto the bench, taking the very edge of one side. It worked okay, but didn't look too comfortable. Her left elbow was on the table, and both feet were on the floor, without her legs going under the table. It looked like she was as much standing on her legs as sitting. So she had to eat sideways, with her back to the cafeteria.

Joey told his boys to sit.

Wayne laughed.

"I'm not sitting with her!" one of the unnamed boys protested.

"I'm not eating with no pig!" said another unnamed boy.

But Joey gave them this look that made them sit anyways. He sat across from Lara, and the others lined up along Joey's side of the table, like birds on a telephone wire. "You can sit all the way on your bench now," Joey said, with his mouth full of burger and bun and ketchup.

Lara smiled at the row of boys, then scooted more onto the bench.

Wayne was telling a joke so loud that I couldn't hear whatever Joey and Lara were saying to each other.

Then the conflict happened.

I don't think Wayne had even eaten one bite of his

food. The unnamed characters were about half done with theirs. Joey did something—like a kick under the table, or maybe some word clue I couldn't hear. But all at once, like they were those swimmers who perform dances in the water and do everything at the same time, Joey and his boys got up. They just stood up and climbed off the bench like they were bailing off a see-saw. And just like that, their end of the table flew up.

And Lara's crashed to the ground. Trays of food slid down the table on top of Lara. The whole table tipped over, and part of it landed on her. She crawled away from it, pushing down on her green dress, which was covered in milk and lettuce and applesauce and pork 'n beans.

Wayne laughed first. He was so loud that the whole entire school ran over to see. Kids shouted, "Look! She's got food all over her!" "She tipped the table!" "I'm glad *I* wasn't sitting there!" And other things that will not be in this book.

Mr. Gray, the janitor, ran over to help, and so did Ms. Cox, the monitor, and even one of the cooks, who still had her plastic hairnet on.

Lara just sat there for a minute, like she didn't know where she was. For just a second, I thought I saw a tear slide down her cheek, but it might could have been the applesauce. Then all of a sudden her smile came back. "I'm okay," she said. But I could see her leg was bleeding.

"What happened?" Ms. Cox demanded.

"I guess I just slid off," Lara answered.

They helped her up. It looked like she couldn't put her weight on one foot all the way. So she limped to the nurse's office, with Ms. Cox and Mr. Gray, one on each arm.

When she came back to our room, she had one leg all Band-Aided up. And she had another poem. I didn't know this until school was all the way over. I had to stay after class and explain to Mrs. Smith how come I hadn't turned in my math homework. Instead of telling the truth, that Matt tore it up and ripped out a whole handful of pages from the math book, too, when I told him I was too busy to make him a chocolate milk shake, I told her I was sorry and would make it up. She believed me because, like I told you, I'm a good actress.

When I left our class, the hallway was almost empty. Joey should have been on the bus already, bossing bus riders around. But instead, he was yelling at Lara. I don't think I described Joey Gilbert's outsides, even though he's more than a minor character. He was wearing a plain white T-shirt and jeans that looked a size too big for him. He's taller than me, but shorter than Wayne and Eric. He always looks tan, and the skin on his forehead is too tight. He has a buzz cut that's so short it's hard to tell what color his hair is. I'm not sure, but I think it's brown. Describing words are adjectives, and here are some for Joey Gilbert: scrappy, wiry, tough, lean, mean. (Those last two rhyme, and that was just on accident.)

"You don't know anything about it, you fat pig!" Joey screamed.

Lara smiled at him.

"Mind your own business! You'd be the last person I'd ask to help me with anything!"

Lara smiled again.

"Just shut the funny up, you sleeveless sweatshirt!" Joey shouted, only with other words. He threw something down and stormed off, hollering at Wayne to hold the bus. I tried to press against the hall wall so as Lara didn't see me seeing her. But it didn't work.

She smiled at me. Then she turned and shuffled away.

In the middle of the hall I could see what Joey had thrown down. And I could see that it was a big wad of paper. I waited until Lara was all the way gone. Then I looked both ways and ran to where Joey had been screaming at Lara. I snatched up the wad of paper, even though it wasn't none of my business and I usually stay out of what's not my business.

Here is what it said:

> *Joey Gilbert, I'm not mad.*
> *I just think you're very sad.*
> *Maybe you still miss your dad?*
> *Miss the love you never had?*
> *Joey, it will be okay,*
> *If you try out for the play.*
> *I could help you learn your part.*
> *The backstage crew could use your art.*
> *Don't pretend that you don't care.*
> *You can do what you can dare.*

When I was almost home, I pulled the note out of my pocket and read it again. Lara was right about Joey's art. He goofed around more than anybody in art class. But his pictures had always been the ones teachers put up on their bulletin boards. I remembered how when we had to draw the part of outside we could see out of our second-grade window, Joey's sky looked exactly like the real sky. He put in the tops of trees and left out the parking lot. And I remembered how I'd wished his picture was something I did because I had just tried to draw the parking lot and my cars looked like ugly bugs.

But I didn't know how Lara knew Joey was good at art.

I also didn't know how she knew about Joey's dad. Robert told me that Joey's dad was a no good son of a spitter, who left when Joey was not even in school yet. And he took the time to beat up Joey's mother before he left, and he put her in the hospital. I saw Joey's mother once when she came to pick him up after the principal kicked him out of school for three days for writing not-nice things on the bathroom wall. She still looked beat-up. And she yelled worse things at Joey than he'd written on the walls.

But I didn't think Lara could have found out about the bathroom walls and Joey's mother.

Sometimes it just seemed like Joey Gilbert was one big conflict waiting to happen. We didn't have to wait long.

10

Suspense

Our teacher Mrs. Smith says that every good story has to have some suspense, and not just the scary stories that call themselves "suspense" or "adventure." She made us look up the word in her giant dictionary, which is almost always harder than you'd think. And it was this time.

I looked up *suspense*, which is tough enough to do because that dictionary has a hundred million words that start with s. Then the dictionary person had this for a definition: "an exciting apprehension to an approaching climax." Which was not any help at all.

So I had to look up *apprehension* and *approaching* (even though I was pretty sure about that one, and I was right) and *climax* (which I'm still not sure about, although there is a chapter coming up by the name "Climax." So maybe you can have suspense wondering what goes on in there).

Looking up *apprehension* made me have to look up other words, like *anticipation*. And this is almost always what happens when Mrs. Smith makes us look up words in her dictionary.

So it took me a very long time to get it. *Suspense* really means that you're kind of afraid because you don't know what's going to happen, but you know that nine times out of ten times, it's going to be a bad thing.

Like when I ended that last chapter like this: "Sometimes it seemed like Joey Gilbert was one big conflict waiting to happen. We didn't have to wait long." I'll bet you weren't thinking that a good thing was going to happen. You knew that something bad was coming. That's suspense.

But it's not going to happen in this chapter, so you can relax.

Now I'm back to the place where I ought to be in the story, and it's Wednesday. On Wednesday, Mrs. Smith finished up reading the whole entire *Fair Day* to us. It was a pretty good play, and it even had some suspense, although none of the scary suspense. Most of the boys would have liked it better if it had had scary suspense. Especially Joey Gilbert, who kept saying stuff like, "This is boring!" and "That's stupid!"

At the end of the play, all the characters are onstage. It's this big fair. And Tom asks Adeline to ride the Ferris wheel with him. And he gives her this stuffed bear he won by busting balloons with darts. She finally says yes she will ride the Ferris wheel with him. And I have to admit that Joey was right about that part because it is kind of lame. But it's also the place where there's suspense because we don't know if she's going to forgive Tom for what she thought he did. It turns out he didn't really do it, but her friend lied to her about it. But Adeline forgives Tom anyway, even though he really didn't do anything, and she takes the bear and heads for the Ferris wheel with him. The end.

Mrs. Smith didn't ask us what part we wanted to try out for in the play. She's pretty smart and probably knew we'd all want to be Adeline or Tom. So she and Ms. Connolly, the other fourth-grade teacher, had it worked out that we would all read Adeline's or Tom's part. Then they'd hear enough to know who should be those parts and who should be the other parts and who should stay back behind the stage and hang up scenery.

Mrs. Smith passed out two pages of script to all of us. Every single one of us took the script, even Larger-than-life Lara. And even Joey Gilbert, who had griped all week about how stupid this was. The script looked like this:

Tom: "What's the matter with you?"
Adeline: "Me? Nothing's the matter with me. But I want you to know that I know what you and Elizabeth have been doing behind my back."
Tom: "What? I don't know what you're talking about, Adeline."

And that's how it went, trading lines between those two main characters.

"You'll have tonight to work on your lines," Mrs. Smith said. "Try to memorize them, as much as you can. I'll give you class time today, too. Ms. Connolly's class will be doing the same thing, and we'll hold tryouts together tomorrow. She and I will assign the parts after tryouts. We only have three weeks to rehearse, to make our scenery, and to get the word out."

"Who's going to come to our stupid play?" asked Joey.

Wayne laughed.

"The other elementary students, for one," Mrs. Smith answered. "Your parents and brothers and sisters and grandparents."

I knew my brothers wouldn't come to the play if I promised to make their beds for a year. I would have liked for my daddy to see me onstage and maybe get the idea for himself that I would be a good actress when I got out of school. But I didn't know if he'd come either.

For the rest of the day, we were supposed to pair off with a partner and practice learning our lines for the tryouts. I hate when we pair off with partners because unless Theresa and Amanda are mad at each other, I never have anybody to partner with. And they weren't mad at each other.

I watched the other kids trade desks and divide up like Noah's ark animals, two by two. Then I saw that Lara and I were the only unpartnered girls, and Eric was the only boy by himself.

"Hey! Hillbilly face!" Eric shouted, dancing up to me. "Practice with me!"

Normally, I would have told Eric to shut his face, and maybe some other things that wouldn't have made it into this book. But seeing's how my only other choice was Lara, I said, "Okay, rat breath."

Eric tried to sit on the floor beside my desk, but he couldn't keep still. "What's the matter with you?" he asked, his voice sounding funny, like a hammer hitting wood.

"Nothing," I snapped, thinking he was making fun because maybe I looked as nervous as I was. "What's wrong with *you?*"

"That's the first line, dumbhead," Eric explained.

I looked at my script. "Oh yeah." Then I read Adeline's first line: "Me? Nothing's the matter with me. But I want you to know that I know what you and Elizabeth have been doing behind my back."

All around the room, I heard the exact same words being said by different voices. It made me think of what an echo in a fun house might sound like.

Eric read Tom's next line. He was a pretty bad reader, which I already knew from when we had reading class. When he said Tom's words, all the words had the same loudness, kind of like a robot.

I went on with the rest of the script, all about how Adeline, which was me, thought Tom, which was Eric, was cheating on her with Elizabeth because Elizabeth had told Adeline that Tom wanted to ride the rides with *her*, that is, Elizabeth.

"This is so lame!" Eric complained.

"Shut up and read your lines," I said.

"I need to go to the bathroom."

Eric went to the bathroom.

I glanced over at Lara. She was reading Mrs. Smith's copy of the whole play. I figured she must have decided not to try out after all, which was probably a good decision because Joey wasn't finished with his conflict.

Eric came back from the bathroom. Then he went to the pencil sharpener. Then he went to see how Joey and Wayne were doing. Then he went to the pencil sharpener again.

I was going to have to learn my lines all by myself when I got home, which I knew could be a big, fat problem.

"What the deuce's devil do you think you're up to?" My middle big brother, Matt, sneaked up on me in the living room.

I had come home to an empty house right after school and curled up on the living-room couch to learn my lines. I was surprised to see how it was almost dark outside. That's how hard I'd been trying to memorize, not that it had done me much good. Adeline's words refused to stick to my brain.

"Where's Luke?" I asked, not answering Matt's question on purpose because he could tear up a script faster than a math book. And it would matter more.

"How the fiery blazes should I know?" Matt turned on the TV and headed for the couch. I escaped before he sat on top of me.

I looked out the front window at the dark shadows over our lawn. Luke should have been home. I would have called Daddy, except for he should have been home, too, and I didn't know where to call him.

I spent about fifteen minutes worrying before I saw Daddy's truck drive up, and Luke got out. When they came in through the kitchen, Luke was crying, and Daddy was yelling at him. "You get to your room!" Daddy shouted. "And if I ever catch you doing that again, you won't be able to get. You hear?"

Luke ran by me, bumping into me in the doorway. He was still crying, and he didn't look up at me.

This is the kind of trouble I don't mess in. So I can't tell you what happened to Luke. Or why our daddy picked him up and brought him home late. And if that makes for suspense, then you should know straight up that you're not going to find out in this book. And I'm just sorry about that. But that's the way it is.

Matt made himself scarce. In the kitchen, Daddy slammed things. Cupboards, fridge, drawers.

I tiptoed up to my room and tried to memorize lines. But I might as well have been out hunting snipes. I fell asleep trying to learn Adeline.

When I woke up, I still had my clothes on. My script was wrinkled under one leg. I changed some of my clothes, washed up, grabbed my wrinkled script, and ran all the way to school in the dark before dawn.

I have this secret place behind the school, outside the backstage door. Sometimes when Daddy's been drinking, or Matt's meaner than usual, I go there and do homework. Or not. Sometimes I just sit on the step and maybe think about being an actress and moving to New York City or Hollywood.

That's where I headed now—not New York City or Hollywood. My secret step. I needed to practice. Today was tryouts, the day when my whole future could get decided. I ran around behind the school and slipped past the big evergreen bush.

In all my years at Paris Elementary, I never saw even one single person besides me sitting on that step. Only today there was. Larger-than-life Lara. I thought about turning around and looking for a new secret spot. But

Lara must have seen me standing there. "Hi, Laney," she said. "Want your spot back?"

"How did you know—?" I started.

She scooted over, like *she* was going to share *my* step with *me*. "Did you get your lines memorized?"

I looked down at my script and shook my head. It made me mad to have her ask this. So I said, kind of meanlike, "Did *you?*" Because I had already figured that she quit, since she didn't look at that script very long in our classroom.

"I did," Lara said.

That surprised me. And if I didn't want to put in one more cliché here, I would say that it took the wind out of my sails.

"Could you use some last-minute help, Laney?" she asked.

I wanted to scream at her that it wasn't fair she could learn her lines so fast and I'd tried and tried and couldn't remember any of them. I wanted to shove her face in, with that smile that was still there, when I couldn't rightly remember the last time I'd smiled.

She patted the step. "Come on. I'll read Tom's lines."

"Won't do any good." I sat on the very edge of my step, as far away from her as I could get on that step. I looked around real quick to make sure nobody saw me sit next to Larger-than-life Lara. I knew that people like Maddie Simpson had to be careful who they sit themselves next to. Their reputations are at stake. And I almost understood why Maddie, in all the five years we went to school together, had never ever once sat herself next to me. What I hadn't figured on before right then was that a person like me had to think about this same thing. And I didn't like that feeling. But that was the way it was.

Lara started right out. Without looking at the script, she said Tom's line: "What's the matter with you?"

I closed my eyes and hoped that that overnight thing had happened to me, like when people say they slept on it and in the morning it came to them. I thought maybe that would happen to me. I had slept on that script. Maybe it had finally worked its way into my brain.

"Nothing's wrong . . . with me," I said, as Adeline. But I knew that wasn't exactly right. And worrying about what I left out kept me from remembering what came next. "Oh, I don't know," I said as myself.

Lara said the whole Adeline line, and she didn't leave out anything. Then she said Tom's next line, without looking at the script. And when I couldn't come up with Adeline's words, she came up with those, too.

"How do you do that?" I asked, so worked up I didn't know whether to cry or scream my head off.

Lara gave me that smile. "Think of it as a poem, Laney."

I got a little apprehension then, which means I got scared of what might be coming next. I thought she might whip out one of her poems on me, and who knows what she could say. Instead, she went on, "Not all poems rhyme. But they all have rhythm, and that's what makes them easy to memorize. A long time ago, people sang history in ballads so ordinary people who couldn't read could pass down that history."

I still didn't know what this had to do with me getting Adeline's words into my head. "So what? I asked, again, kind of meanlike.

"Listen to the lines, Laney," she said. "Hear the rhythm." She repeated the lines, the same lines I'd been pounding my brain to get into my head. But when she said the words, they came out different. They sounded more like music. Or a boat, rocking side to side in little waves on the ocean.

"How did you do that?" I asked, when she'd done it to the whole entire tryout script, all by heart.

"It's easy. Look." She took my wrinkled script and divided Adeline's lines so it looked like this, for example:

But I want / you to know / that I know /
what you / and Eli / zabeth have / been doing / behind
my back.

Since you are just reading the words, you can't hear them like I did. But take my word for it that those divided-up words made perfect sense when she was saying them in that rocking way. It made the lines sound like a song that's got stuck in your head.

So maybe that explains what happened next because I can't explain it in other ways. I read the lines like Lara had divided them up. Then she said Tom's part. And when I got to Adeline's next lines, I could say them without looking. It was like I could still hear them rocking. I could hear Lara's voice, hear it larger than life.

By then it was full light. I heard a bus come up School Road, and I knew it was Joey Gilbert's bus. And even though Lara had just helped me take the most biggest step toward my only dream in life, I hopped up off that step faster than bees sneeze. And I ran around the building, just as that bus was pulling up.

But in the window of that bus, there was Joey Gilbert. He was frowning out at me. And for one terrible moment, I was sure he'd seen me with Larger-than-life Lara and that I wouldn't never hear the end of it.

11

Cliffhangers

Joey Gilbert didn't see me and Lara on the secret step.

I let you think that he maybe did because that's a writing trick that Mrs. Smith taught us about. It's called the "Cat in the Alley" trick. I love that, the "Cat in the Alley" name. But *trick* isn't the right word, because it's very fair to use it to get suspense when you tell a story.

The way it works is this. You are inside the house at night. Somebody crazy is after you and has just given you a scary call on the telephone to tell you that he's going to chop off your head. You decide to watch TV to take your mind off things. Then you hear a noise out-side. You turn off the TV sound and listen to be sure. Then there's that noise again. You get scareder and scareder. So you get you a weapon, like a broom or a bat, and you try to be brave. Slowly, you creep to the back door, where you heard the scary noise outside of. You slip out into the alley, with your broom or bat raised over your head. "I know you're out there!" you cry, with a shaky voice because you're so scared. "Come on out or I'm calling the police!" You hold your breath. The readers hold their breath.

Then a cat comes out from behind the trash can.

That is the "Cat in the Alley" trick. And if you keep reading that book for a few pages, that scary guy will probably come back for real. And this time, you will think it's the cat, until the scary guy jumps out at you and really scares you to death.

So Joey Gilbert didn't see me sitting with Lara. But maybe he will next time.

Or maybe not.

I just thought I had to end that chapter, which was called "Suspense," with something like the Cat in the Alley.

● ● ●

Mrs. Smith tried to teach us science in the morning, but it wasn't working for her. You would have thought she had herself one whole entire room full of Eric Radabaughs. Finally, it got to be time to have the try-outs. We followed each other down the hall, getting yelled at the whole way because we were poking each other and laughing and being loud, like we were Wayne Wilson.

Ms. Connolly's room was just as bad, by the way.

Our teachers herded us into the gym, which was also the stage for acting, depending on what you wanted it to be. The whole fourth grade of Paris Elementary sat on the floor, close to the stage, except for that Lara got to sit in a folding chair behind us and so did the principal, who was just along to watch. We were as noisy as locusts.

Mrs. Smith and Ms. Connolly climbed to the stage. Wayne laughed and yelled, "Bravo!" and started everybody, except the principal, clapping. It took them a couple of minutes to shut us up again.

Ms. Connolly had the loudest voice, between her and Mrs. Smith, so she started. "Listen up, people! We better get started. We have a lot of people trying out here today. Now, we've heard all of you sing in music, so we won't be having musical auditions per se. You have your lines. When we call your names, hurry up here on-stage and perform the scene you've all been given.

"So, let's proceed. Mrs. Smith and I have decided that to be fair, we'll start the boys alphabetically, and the girls in reverse alphabetical order."

Seeing as how I'm a G, it didn't matter that much to me, one way or the other.

"No fair!" shouted Joey Gilbert, even though he's also a G.

You could tell our teachers had it all planned out. They called out, "Michael Adams," from Ms. Connolly's room, and "Delaney Wells," from our room, and those two got to go up onstage first. It made me very glad that my name wasn't Laney Zany or something.

Michael and Delaney read Adeline's and Tom's speeches to each other. Then they sat down, and two more people got called up.

It got pretty boring after a while. They all kind of sounded alike. Most of them sounded like Eric, with the words coming out like they were robots. Maddie Simpson tossed her wavy, blond hair when she said her lines, and she stuck her tiny nose up in the air. So that was a little different than everybody else. But her words sounded the same. The only other different person was Sara Rivers. When she said Adeline's lines, we all got really still. And I think it was because even though we'd heard the lines so much we wanted to hurl, still, Sara sounded like she was really Adeline and her feelings were really hurt by Tom, instead of by Travis Freeman, who was pretending to be Tom.

There was a long way to go to get to me. I tried to say the lines to myself for practice, when kids said them to each other onstage. Only that didn't work good, because the lines in my head rolled, and theirs didn't.

As the girls' names got closer to the G's, my stomach started feeling like Eric Radabaugh was running around in there.

"Paul Peterson and Laney Grafton," Mrs. Smith announced.

My legs felt cold and tingly as I climbed up to the stage, and I don't think it was because I'd been sitting on them. Paul Peterson was in Ms. Connolly's room, and he was one of the most popular boys in that room. So that didn't help either.

We had to stand on the front part of the stage, where you could see kids staring at you. I think I saw Lara sitting in her chair. But I'm not too sure about that. And the truth of it is that I'm not too sure about anything that happened next. I know Paul said his Tom line. And I think there was this long wait while my mouth caught up to my brain. Then I heard that not-rhyming poem song Lara had made out of Adeline's words, and I said that. Paul said his. I said mine. Tom said his. Adeline said hers. And we were done.

I remember thinking that I must have done all right because nobody was laughing at me or calling me a hillbilly name or anything. Not that I could have heard them anyway. My heart was pounding like my biggest big brother, Robert's, radio before our daddy gets home.

Other kids got up onstage and down onstage. But I was still out in that boat on the ocean, with the waves rocking me back and forth.

We had girl As and boy Zs (David Zeller) read their parts. I figured we must be done. Ms. Connolly must have figured the same thing. "Well, that's wonderful! You should all be very proud of yourselves today."

Mrs. Smith came up to her and touched her arm. Then she stood on tiptoes to talk into her ear. Ms. Connolly looked troubled.

Then Mrs. Smith turned to us on the gym floor and said, "Everybody, stay seated, please. We're not finished yet. We have one more tryout for the part of Adeline.

Lara Phelps. Lara, would you come up here, please? And I apologize for not having you on our list. We were going from our old roster."

Every head turned to watch Lara as she shuffled all the way around the crowd on the floor to get to the stage. I was pretty sure those steps weren't going to be easy on her, and I was right. There were only three steps going up to the stage, but they were big steps.

"Since all the boys have tried out for Tom's part already, do I have a volunteer to read the lines with Lara?" Mrs. Smith asked.

Wayne laughed. Loud.

Mrs. Smith cleared her throat. "It would be a good opportunity to get a second chance at the tryout, in case you didn't like your first attempt."

Nobody raised his hand.

Joey Gilbert was sitting behind me. I heard him tell Eric, who really could have used a second chance, "Don't you dare raise that hand, Radabaugh! You do, and you'll be sorry."

"Well . . ." Mrs. Smith turned to Ms. Connolly. "I guess I could read Tom's part."

"That's okay." Lara had finally gotten herself to the stage. She was breathing hard. But she didn't look scared or anything, and I think the breathing hard was on account of the three steps.

She shuffled toward us, so that she was right on the edge of the stage, looking out.

Behind her, Mrs. Smith said, "But, Lara, you need someone to read Tom's lines."

"It's okay, Mrs. Smith. Thank you." She smiled at the teachers, then smiled at us. Then she turned her head one way and asked, "What's the matter with you?"

She turned her head the other way, and in this soft voice said, "Me? Nothing's the matter with me. But I want you to know that I know what you and Elizabeth have been doing behind my back."

She turned back and lowered her voice. "What? I don't know what you're talking about, Adeline."

And she went on like that, saying both parts, making us believe she was both Adeline and Tom. Making us believe we were at the fair and didn't want nothing except for Adeline and Tom to get together for that Ferris wheel ride.

When she was done, I had to stop myself from clapping. Nobody clapped. But nobody called her a fat pig either. And every kid in the whole fourth grade had paid attention. Lara Phelps crossed the stage and waddled down the steps and back to her chair before the teachers said anything.

Then Mrs. Smith broke out into a big smile. "Well. That was . . . amazing. I don't think there's any doubt who's earned the part of Adeline here today. I think I can speak for both fourth-grade teachers when I say the lead role in *Fair Day* goes to—"*

---

*This is called a cliffhanger. It got its name from old movies, where you'd have the hero or heroine get pushed off a cliff and just barely grab on to the cliff to keep from falling down and dying dead and the scene would end. And the hero or heroine would hang there and wait to get rescued. So he or she was hanging from a cliff. The end of that scene, with him or her hanging from a cliff, got called a cliffhanger. And that's what I did to end this chapter, which goes by the name "Cliffhanger." Nobody is actually dangling from a cliff, but you know what I mean.

12

Twist

"Wait a minute, Mrs. Smith," Ms. Connolly interrupted. "I think we need to confer and select all the roles, as we planned. Don't you?"

"Well . . ." Mrs. Smith began.

Ms. Connolly took over again and talked to us kids, who were back to sounding like locusts. "We'll have the results of the tryouts printed up for you tomorrow. We'll post the roles and actors and actresses outside each of the fourth-grade rooms, as well as the names of set designers and stage managers, which are also very important roles in our production. Let's keep it down as we go back to our rooms!"

The school bell rang, which meant we were done with school.

"And again!" Ms. Connolly shouted. "Thank you all for coming! You're all winners! Quietly, boys and girls!"

So we didn't find out who got to be what in our play that Thursday. And maybe that was the beginning of the twist. Mrs. Smith says a plot twist is when you expect something to happen, but something else happens instead. And that is what happened when we got to school on Friday.

Here is what I expected, and I think most kids expected:

- Lara Phelps won the part of Adeline.
- Some kids maybe even thought she won the Tom part, too, on account of her having read his part better than Paul or Carlos or T.J. But I didn't think this because it would be too hard for her to kiss herself in the end of the story and take a stuffed bear from her own self and walk off toward the Ferris wheel, hand in hand, when they were both her hands. Whoever ended up playing Tom

was going to raise a big, fat stink about having to pretend to be in love with big, fat Lara.

- There would be a lot of crying by the girls who didn't win.
- There would be a lot of yelling by the teachers who wanted us to believe that all of the parts were important and we shouldn't feel bad about drawing the background scenery.
- There would be a lot of laughing at everybody from Wayne Wilson.
- Joey Gilbert would say that everything was "No fair!"

There was one more thing I expected, but I didn't put it on my expected list for two reasons. One, it is about me, and I'm just a minor character. And two, I'm not sure if it was an expected thing or more like a big, fat hope. I thought I maybe would get a part in the play for real. And I knew it would be because of Lara Phelps and the way she divided up the lines and turned them into a poem song that didn't rhyme.

Friday morning, everybody who could showed up early for class. I thought I would be the first one there, but I was number seven.

Sara Rivers was the first one I heard. She was standing with the other kids, who were pushing at each other to read the tryout lists. "I won!" Sara shouted. "I can't believe it! I'm Adeline!"

So that was the first plot twist. Because although Sara was probably second best, she wasn't as good as Lara was. Amanda and Ashley and some of the other girls—Maddie Simpson was not there yet—were acting all excited for Sara. Ashley cried, "Oh, I just knew you'd get it, Sara."

Only she couldn't have. Nobody could have known that. It was a twist.

I saw Maddie trotting up the hall. You could tell that she thought she was going to see her own name as the star on that list.

"Here she comes," Becca whispered. She and Maddie had been best friends in third grade. So she knew enough about Maddie Simpson to know what was coming was not going to be good.

Sara waved at Maddie. The pinkish went out of her cheeks. "Maddie, I—I mean, I'm sorry—"

Wayne laughed. "You didn't get the part, Maddie!" he shouted. "Sara did!"

"What?" Maddie looked like she couldn't believe this twist in her plans. "Where?"

The crowd parted so she could pass through to the tryout sheets. She stood there reading those names. She could have read the whole, entire dictionary during the time she read those names. Finally, she said, "This can't be right." Without a word to her best friend, Sara, she stormed into our classroom, shouting out, "Mrs. Smith!"

I walked up to the lists. Nobody seemed to notice I was there. I read Sara's name next to "Adeline." So I saw that for myself. Carlos's name was next to Tom. This was not as big of a twist because Carlos was the best of the boys in the boy part.

Then I saw my own name.

Now I got to admit that early on in this chapter I talked big. I learned this from my brothers. All of them. I said I expected to get a part in the play. But the truth is that I was hoping so hard, it just felt like expecting. And by the time I got home, it was back to just hoping, without any expecting mixed in. And by the time I went to bed, there wasn't even much hoping left. And when I got up this morning, I was expecting again. Only this time, I was expecting NOT to get a part in the play because I should have known, like my daddy knows, that Graftons don't get parts in plays.

Only get this. I got a part.

Next to "Laney Grafton" was "Caroline." I remembered that part when Mrs. Smith read that whole play to us. Caroline was a girl who brings her pigs to the fair to be judged. Only she doesn't want them to win after all because that means her dad would kill them all dead, and she thinks this one is really a pet. Anyway, she was in the play a whole lot and had a lot of lines. Maybe next to Adeline and Elizabeth, Caroline said more than any other girl in the whole entire play.

So that was really a twist because I didn't think I would ever really get that part.

More kids came and crowded around the tryout list. Some girls started crying because they didn't get parts. And this was no twist because it's what I thought would happen. The boys didn't cry. But they put up a big stink.

"Hey! That's no fair!" Joey Gilbert shouted. He'd marched straight off his bus and shoved his way to the front of the crowd. "I don't want to be a spitting, crummy scenery guy!" But he didn't raise as big a stink as he would have if he'd gotten Tom's part and Lara had gotten Adeline's.

Which brings me back to the biggest twist. Lara's name was not next to any of the characters in the whole play. She did not win a single part. Instead, she was on the bottom sheet with kids like Eric Radabaugh and Wayne Wilson and unnamed boys and girls from Ms. Connolly's class. They were all lumped together under "Stage Crew."

I ducked out of the crowd and went into my class-room. Carly and Stephanie were crying together on one side of the room. Lara was sitting behind her desk on the other side of the room, and Mrs. Smith looked like she was talking important things to her.

But Maddie wouldn't let that happen. "Why didn't I get to be Adeline? Everybody said I should be! You just ask them. I don't want to be Elizabeth!"

"Stop shouting, Maddie," Mrs. Smith said.

"I *won't* stop! And my parents are going to be really mad when they hear about this. This is *so* not fair!"

"The only not-fair thing is that Lara didn't win." I was the one who said this, which was a twist on me because I never ever mess in trouble that's not any of my business.

Mrs. Smith and Maddie turned to look at me. They looked as surprised to hear me say this as I was to hear me say this.

Mrs. Smith's face looked like she slept in it. It was the most wrinkliest I'd ever seen it. "Laney," she began, "I was just trying to explain how we arrived at this de-cision. Lara absolutely did the best at tryout. I don't think there's any doubt about that."

"Hey!" Maddie interrupted. "Wait just a darn minute!"

"Maddie, please!" Mrs. Smith snapped. "Take your seat." Maddie spun on her heels and huffed back to her desk. Mrs. Smith went on. "Ms. Connolly felt Lara was just too new to Paris. Neither of us has heard her sing. And then there's the entire cast to consider. Who will work well with whom . . . well, it's really quite complicated. I know it might not seem—" She broke off here, and her voice cracked. She swallowed hard, and her eyes got all watery.

Then that thing happened again. Lara got her smile, and this is what she said to Mrs. Smith:

> "Mrs. Smith, it's all okay.
> Please don't worry for this play.
> Things can always work out best,
> Sometimes life is just a test.
> I can understand—you bet!
> Besides, I'll like to work on set."

And that was the last real twist. Because there were Lara Phelps and Mrs. Smith. But instead of Lara crying and the teacher trying to make her feel better, it was twisted the other way around.

13
Details

The next three weeks at Paris Elementary were full up with regular school stuff, plus the play. At my house, it took some very good acting for me to keep going to practices. And another thing was that my littlest big brother, Luke, never said what had made him cry that day. In fact, he didn't say nothing. He stopped talking altogether, as far as I could see.

Robert and Matt never noticed. I said something to Daddy about it one night, but he told me to worry about my own business. So you'd think that having one of my three brothers not talking or calling me mean names would have been a good thing. But it didn't feel like it was a good thing.

Three weeks is a whole long time to cover when you're writing a book, unless it's a book that goes on and on about a person's whole entire life, which this book does not. If I told you about every single play practice, and every single meanness done to Lara, or every single fight my two talking brothers got themselves into, this part of the book could be really boring, which I don't want to happen.

Mrs. Smith says you can't never write about every single thing that happens. So what you got to do is pick the right details that give the best picture. "Details, details, details!" That's Mrs. Smith's favorite cheer.

There is an example about details that has to do with the play, *Fair Day*. And so I will use that. Joey Gilbert really got into painting the scenery and background decoration stuff, once he stopped saying "Unfair!" to everything. Only he was trying to draw and paint a whole entire fairgrounds, including stuff like a green field and empty animal pens and the road in front of the fairgrounds and the places between the chicken barn and the rabbit cages.

So Mrs. Smith said, "Joey, these are wonderful

paintings. But we just need the *details* of our setting. If you give us a Ferris wheel, a roller coaster, one or two games, like the balloon dart game, and a couple of other details, the audience will fill in the rest." And I thought that was very good advice.

So I will give you some details of the three weeks we practiced for our play. Only this is harder than you might think. So I'm doing what Mrs. Smith made us do when we started studying details. We did two exercises that lasted one day for each exercise. And this was the first one: Tell about your day, but you can only use verbs, which are action words. Here is my three weeks from the time I got the part to the day of the play.

Classroom
Tried (to listen)
Fell (asleep)
Failed (a test)
Shut (up)
Shouted (at Joey)
Watched (Lara)
Wrote (some of this)
Divided (up Caroline's lines in the play)
Memorized

Other people in my class
Laughed
Made fun
Poked
Whispered
Pointed
Practiced
Griped
Drew (on big poster board)
Blew up (balloons)
Built
Painted
Talked (to one another)

Larger-than-life Lara
Smiled
Helped
Suggested
Worked
Carried
Complimented
Hummed
Shuffled
Ate (alone)

Sat (alone)
Smiled

People in my house
Yelled
Cursed
Fought (over TV)
Hit
Hit back
Shoved
Slammed
Shouted
Complained
Threatened
Kicked
Dodged
Fought (over bathroom)
Punched
Punched back
Swore
Left

The second exercise Mrs. Smith made us do so we
could learn about details was very much like that first

exercise, but you could only use nouns. Nouns are names of things that are people, places, or things. Only I'm not going to do so much with this exercise for these reasons. First, I ended up writing down a lot of details in verbs and that took up a lot of space in this chapter. Second, I don't want it to be boring, going over the same thing. Third, I'm tired of these exercises.

So here are three weeks of nouns.

Lara

Joey Gilbert

[All the other nouns that are names of people I already told you about, I won't put here. Just so you know, these nouns are called "proper" and they have capital letters on them.]

Paris Elementary

desk

pencil

test

grade

61% [This is a number, but I think it's a noun, too, although I'm not sure about that.]

trash can

script

stuffed pigs

balloons

Ferris wheel

bell

practice

lines

mistakes

practice

darkness

rain

speed

mud

fear

house

porch

door

DADDY

shouts [This can be a noun or a verb, which is con-
fusing. And there are other words in this list like
that.]

clock

words (bad)

beer

Daddy

hand

slap [This is another of those words that is a noun and a verb.]

Laney

cheek

tears

stairs

bed

wish

prayer

sleep

I'm done with these exercises and with this chapter because sometimes you just don't want to give any more details.

14

Transition

That last chapter was really hard to write. And I had to leave a lot of things out, of which some, I think, were important. You could read all of those verbs and nouns and still not get it that the teasing of Larger-than-life Lara didn't let up. But it didn't. It got worse. Or better, depending on how you look at it. Ms. Connolly and Mrs. Smith were always telling us how all our play practices were going to make us better at acting the play. And that's kind of like the way all the practice teasing Lara Phelps just made Joey Gilbert and everybody better at it. Meaner.

So just because I didn't keep up that part of the story, don't forget it.

Because I have to get this story up to the dress rehearsal. To do this, I need what Mrs. Smith calls a transition, which is a fancy way of saying that you're getting from someplace to another place without stopping everywhere in between. Transitions keep things from getting too long, which is why this chapter is very short. I had to skip over stuff like I did about that teasing getting worse. I also had to skip most of what went on at my house before dress-rehearsal day, except for one thing.

Something funny was that I'd taken to talking more to my littlest big brother, Luke. He didn't talk back. He still wasn't talking. But after about a week of me talking to him for a change, he stopped slamming his bedroom door in my face. Sometimes he would just stay where he was, like in the living room or maybe at the kitchen table eating Chinese chow mein, which is something he can eat cold and out of the can. And I would sit by him, if I didn't get too close, and tell him about Larger-than-life Lara and Joey Gilbert. I still hadn't talked to my daddy about the play since that night I asked him if I could try out for it. He never talked about it either. There had been a few times when he got really mad at me for getting home late and not having groceries to eat or clean clothes for him to wear. And you read about one of those times in that list of nouns, but you may not have noticed.

I never said one word about the play to my brothers, and I think you can figure out why that was. But I was getting used to talking to my littlest big brother, Luke. So two nights before the play, when we were the only ones home, we were sitting in the kitchen. Luke was eating three hot dogs that he didn't even bother to make hot, so they were more like cold dogs.

And I said, "Luke, I'm going to be an actress."

He choked on his dog, so I knew he heard me.

"Our class is putting on a play. And it's called *Fair Day*. And I tried out for a part in that play, and I won one. I memorized all the lines. And that's where I've been all these times when I'm not at our house."

I stopped and hoped maybe that would shock him so much that he'd talk. But he didn't. Which, I admit, took care of one worry. And that was that he'd tell Robert or Matt. "The play is Friday night," I went on. "We have dress rehearsal tomorrow afternoon, which means we act out the whole entire play, but only for ourselves, but we've got to wear our play costumes, of which I don't have one of exactly. I'm wearing jeans and a shirt."

Luke didn't get up and go away.

"I'm real scared about that play, Luke. But I'm excited about it, too, because I think I'll be an actress. And you could come if you want."

Luke looked up from his hot dog. His eyes aren't slanty like Robert's and Matt's and Daddy's. He has big brown eyes, that for the first time I thought looked like my eyes. He stared at me for probably a whole entire minute. I stared him back.

Then he stood up and walked out of the room.

15

Rising Action

The next day after Luke didn't talk to me was our dress rehearsal. I had a funny feeling on that day. It felt like I was on a sled and flying down a steep hill and couldn't stop. And somehow, I knew there was a crash waiting at the bottom of that hill. That's what that felt like.

Mrs. Smith says that in a story you got your rising action and your falling action. I never understood that part very good. And this is why. Rising action is like when you're creeping toward something big that's going to happen. So you're stepping closer to it, and I guess you could think of it like you're climbing up a ladder. And that makes sense about the rising part of this action. Falling action would be coming down from the ladder, after the big thing happened on top of it.

So that's probably how it got its name of "rising" action. And you are supposed to have some of that before you get to the climax, where the really, really big action thing happens. Only I think that it feels more like a sliding-down-the-hill action. You go faster and faster and faster all the way to the *crash*, which is waiting for you at the bottom of the hill. And that's more what it felt like on the day before the play, when we had to have our dress rehearsal. It felt like we were all on a sled and picking up speed.

Rising action the day of dress rehearsal started with us practicing in our classroom. I still pretty much practiced my Caroline speeches by myself, which was no problem because the real Caroline in *Fair Day* spent most of her time with her pigs. She had one favorite pig, which was by the name of Hamlet. And that is kind of a play on words because "ham" comes from dead pigs. And Caroline wouldn't "let" her daddy kill her pig. Plus, *Hamlet* was a real, live play written by Shakespeare, who wrote in hard English. So that was a very good name for that pig.

Theresa brought in a stuffed pig the size of her dog. I had seen this stuffed pig when I was at Theresa's house, when her and Amanda were being mad at each other. Theresa's whole room was pink like that pig. So I asked her could I borrow that pig in the play. And she said I could, but I better take real good care of it. And I said I would and that at least her pig would get to be in the play, which I thought was a thing to say to make her feel better because Theresa didn't have herself a part in the play. Only Theresa didn't like that I said that. But she still let me use her pig, as long as I took good care of it.

Then Sara Rivers, all by herself, brought in eleven stuffed pigs for Caroline because it turns out Sara collects pigs.

So I was saying my lines to Hamlet. But I was watching Lara, too.

Lara Phelps moved around our classroom as fast as her legs could go. She cut out the drawings on poster board because nobody else wanted to do that. She glued felt onto the Ferris wheel because Eric Radabaugh kept getting glue all over everything, and that includes himself and the pencil sharpener, which Mrs. Smith said would never sharpen again. And because Wayne Wilson kept sniffing that glue until Lara took it over. She was the one who swept the stage after school, too.

I first felt that sled take off downhill when I saw Wayne Wilson whispering to Joey Gilbert. And this was not Wayne's regular whisper that sounds like a normal person's talk. He was whispering for real, so as I couldn't make out a word of it. And there was a lot of this kind of whispering going on in our room, even though Mrs. Smith was letting us talk out loud so we could say our play lines to each other. In addition to Wayne Wilson and Joey Gilbert, other whisperers were: Roger Steeby and two unnamed boys from Ms. Connolly's class, who were helpers with making scenery. Maddie Simpson, Carly, Kaitlyn, Jordan, Amy, Felicia, and Hannah, and maybe some others I forgot.

There was secret laughing going on, too, where you couldn't figure out what they were laughing at. And if you asked nicely, "What's so funny?" they gave you mean looks and said stuff like:

"Shut up."

"*You're* what's so funny, hillbilly!" (Only you knew that this was a lie this time.)

"Mind your own business, Laney."

So like I said, I was practicing with Theresa's big pig: "Don't worry, Hamlet. In all the world there could never be a pig as lovely as you." When I said these lines, I divided them up in my head so they sounded like a poem song that doesn't rhyme. And it went like this:

> Don't worry, Hamlet. /
> In all the world / there could never be
> a pig as lovely as you. /

I could sing that poem to you, if you could do that in a book.

"I need that pig!" Joey Gilbert grabbed Hamlet's pig head and yanked. I grabbed the pig's belly just in time. "Stop it!" I shouted.

"Shhhh!" Joey whispered, which was a very strange thing to hear Joey telling somebody else to shhhh. "I'll give it back."

I didn't let go. First, I needed that pig. Second, it was Theresa's pig, and I promised to take good care of it. Third, Joey is a liar, and he probably wouldn't never give that pig back.

"Oh, all right!" Joey let go of Hamlet, and I fell down on my backside.

And that sled kept going faster and faster down that hill.

The true thing is that I didn't worry much about Joey Gilbert doing that with Hamlet. And this was because Joey Gilbert is the kind of boy who grabs things from people for no good reason.

Only a little while later, I saw Joey drawing pigs—lots and lots of pigs—onto poster board. Maddie and her friends were coloring those pigs pink with markers and crayons. And other girls than Lara were cutting those pigs out.

And there was another thing. Balloons. Wayne and Eric and a bunch of kids kept bringing in bags of balloons, like they were one big, fat balloon factory.

Mrs. Smith strolled back to the balloon corner and looked real surprised to see all those balloons there. "I think we have more than enough balloons for the fair," she told them.

Maddie smiled up at her. "We thought they'd make good decorations on the ceiling over the stage."

"Shouldn't you be practicing Elizabeth's lines for your scenes, Maddie?" Mrs. Smith asked.

"Yes, Mrs. Smith," said Maddie, all fake syrupy sweet. Plus, she looked like she was a beer breath away from cracking up laughing.

"How's it going, Laney?" Lara stopped beside my desk. She was carrying a big cardboard box, loaded with stage stuff, called props. These were: fake darts, fake fireworks, fake cotton candy, fake flowers, hats, old shoes, and like that.

"It's going okay," I said.

"Need help on your lines?" She shifted the box in her arms.

I shook my head. I thought about telling her that I'd memorized all my lines in two days, on account of I turned them into poem songs that stuck in my head.

"Great!" Lara smiled at me. "I'm really glad you got the part of Caroline," she said.

"You are?" I'd figured she might be real mad at all of us who got parts when we were worse than her saying those lines, and she'd said the parts better than us.

"I think Caroline is the best role in the whole play," Lara continued. "She's the strongest character in *Fair Day*. She knows who she is. She knows what she wants. And she never lets other people throw her off."

I liked Caroline in the play, too. Only I hadn't thought how come.

"Well, good luck, Laney. Break a leg this afternoon!"

I already knew that she wasn't saying I should really

break my leg (which is what Joey Gilbert would have meant if he'd have said this, and he would even have tried to help it happen). "Break a leg" is what actors and actresses say to each other for good luck. Only don't ask me why. One day I'll look it up in the big dictionary, but I don't have that much time yet.

"You, too," I said, meaning Lara should break a leg, too. Only she was already shuffling toward the door, her big box balanced on her belly. Her thighs slapped against each other so it sounded kind of like applause.

Dress rehearsal started after lunch, which must have been a very bad idea because Sara Rivers, Erin McDonald, and Tamara Reno all hurled in the girls' john on the way to the gym.

I admit straight up that I felt like doing this myself. Only I didn't have nothing to throw up on account of I had forgot to pack me a lunch.

Us girls had to change into our costumes in the girls' locker room. I didn't like this any better than when we had to change into our gym clothes. Maddie put on a pink dress that made her look like a princess, instead of Elizabeth, the friend at the fair. Sara wore a blue-and-white-checkered dress, and it made her look just like

Adeline should have looked for that fair. Mrs. Smith said I could wear jeans because Caroline in the story was a farmer, so I did that. And that was a very good thing because I didn't have many other clothes to choose from.

We did our whole dress rehearsal on the stage, with all the drawings and scenery set up and all the lights on and everybody just as nervous like it was the real show. Joey and Wayne and Eric and Roger kept themselves backstage most of the time, and I'm not sure what they did back there. But I kept an eye on all my pigs. Lara carried whole entire sets onstage, like the balloon game and Ferris wheel or the barn and pigpen.

I kept watching for all those balloons and pigs Joey and Wayne had been making up, but I never saw them.

I won't bore you with the rest of what happened at rehearsal because a rehearsal is only just a fancy prac-tice. And the next chapter is the real play. So you will get enough of this stuff then, I promise. Because even though I was sure that action was rising, and Joey and Wayne and Eric and Maddie and everybody were up to something, it didn't happen. We got ourselves through that whole entire dress rehearsal. And that sled that had felt like it was going faster and faster never did crash.

When the whole play was over, every one of us

actors and actresses lined up in front and held hands and bowed. And I was glad I had two girls on the sides of me so I didn't have to hold a boy's hand. When we were done bowing, we stepped back and let all the scenery makers and backstage people hold hands in front of us and take a bow, too. And I thought that was pretty fair.

That night I told my littlest big brother, Luke, about our dress rehearsal. And then I told him about that sled going downhill and how it didn't crash and that I figured that maybe I'd been all wrong about that rising action and that sled sliding.

Only that's when I remembered all those balloons in the corner and those pigs Joey drew and Maddie cut out. And I got that sick, sled-sliding feeling again that I was right about that rising action.

And you would know this for yourself that this was true if you turned the page because that next chapter is called "Climax."

16
Climax

I will skip stuff what happened in school on the day of our play because nothing much did. Mrs. Smith says that the climax of a story is the most importantest part of the story, which is why this chapter is the hardest to write. And if I don't do it right or I forget things, then I'm just sorry about that. But I'm only ten, and as my daddy says, "Laney, you ain't the sharpest knife in the drawer." And I don't think this is a cliché because I never heard anybody's daddy say this a lot, except mine.

I still hadn't come straight out and told my daddy

about *Fair Day* since that first time. Part of this reason was because he'd taken to staying out later and later. This wasn't an entirely bad thing because he didn't get mad so much when I was late on account of he was later.

Mrs. Smith told us to be at the school at 6:30 at night to get ready for the play. At six at night, I was still the only person home in our house. I kept thinking Luke would come home and that he was my best chance to have somebody sitting in our audience because of me.

At 6:13 at night, I wrote my family a note, and it looked like this:

> To Daddy and Robert and Matt and Luke,
> I am Caroline in a play by the name of Fair Day
> tonight. If you want to see me, I'm at school in this
> play.
> It starts at 7:30 at night.
>
> > Bye, Laney
> > P.S. In the gym.

I walked into school at the same exact time as Lara, and this was by accident.

"Laney, you did a great job in rehearsal," Lara said.

"Thanks," I said back. "You, too." Which was dumb

because she hadn't acted. And also I don't know if Lara heard that part. I still wonder about that.

"Where's Joey?" Mrs. Smith asked, when most all of the rest of us were in our classroom. Some kids, like Maddie and Sara, were getting makeup put on them. Others of us, like me and Carlos, were just making sure we were buttoned or zipped up and maybe had our props, such as stuffed pigs.

"Has anyone seen Joey?" Mrs. Smith asked again. "Where are Wayne and Eric?"

"They were here earlier, Mrs. Smith," Sara Rivers answered.

Maddie Simpson poked Sara, and I saw this with my own eyes. Then she said, "They went to the bathroom."

Then Joey and his boys finally came back. And then it got pretty crazy in our room because Carly couldn't find the cotton candy, which was fake and was found in her desk later. And then I couldn't find Sara's little stuffed pigs, except for I did find half of them. And I had Theresa's big, stuffed Hamlet. Then Janelle's fake rabbits were missing. Only she found them where she'd left them, which was in her desk. Only I never could find the other missing pigs that were Sara's.

Mrs. Smith said that we had to go, and that half of Sara's pigs would have to be enough. Only I didn't like this, and it felt like we were starting this play with a bad start. And I couldn't help myself from thinking that I was back on that sled, sliding downhill, and *Fair Day* wasn't even on yet.

All of us actors and actresses marched to the backstage, following Ms. Connolly, with Mrs. Smith bringing up the rear. I felt like we were baby ducks being led to the water so as we could learn to swim. I'll bet those ducks would be both excited and scared at the same time, which is what I was.

There were already some people's parents sitting in the folding chairs set up in the gym. There were a lot of those chairs in that gym, and I couldn't help myself looking at all of them to see if my daddy was in one of them, which he was not.

Backstage, which is a thing you say when you're an actor and you are not on the stage, but just behind the curtain or maybe sideways to people who are, it really did look like a fair. The Ferris wheel turned out so good that even though you couldn't ride it or anything, you knew exactly what it was supposed to be.

My favorite part of the scenery was the pigpen stage left, which seemed like stage right to me. And this is very hard to keep that straight. I put the five little piggies of Sara's into the pen. Then I kissed Theresa's pig,

Hamlet, on its head for good luck and sat him in the pen, too.

Lara was in a different place every time I looked at her. These places were: the balloon-game prop, where she set out arrows and prizes; the front, where she checked the lights; the back, where she moved the Act 2 scenery so you couldn't see it until Act 2.

"Places everyone!" Mrs. Smith hollered. She gave us a five-minute warning and counted down each minute like this: "Four minutes . . . three minutes . . . two minutes . . . one minute . . ."

When she got to zero minutes, she didn't have to shush us on account of we were too scared to talk. The curtain pulled open like the curtains at Theresa's house. This was the cue for Adeline and Elizabeth to come onto the stage from different sides and meet in the middle, under the fake tree. And this is exactly what Adeline (which was really Sara) did. Only when she got to the fake apple tree, Elizabeth wasn't there (which was really Maddie not being there).

Maddie was still backstage beside Mrs. Smith. "I can't do it!" Maddie was saying over and over.

"Of course you can," Mrs. Smith was telling her over and over.

I didn't know which one of them was right about that.

Meanwhile, Sara was doing a very good job of pretending onstage. "Well, I wonder where my best friend, Elizabeth, is," Sara said.

This part was not in the real play called *Fair Day*. This part was not in our dress rehearsal. I didn't know it right then, but that line was made up by Lara Phelps and whispered out to Sara to cover up for Maddie not being there.

Finally, Mrs. Smith gave Maddie a little push that made her be onstage, only not by the apple tree.

"There you are!" Sara said, which was one more line made up by Lara.

"Elizabeth, have you seen Tom?" Sara/Adeline asked. And this was the first real line of the play.

It should have been answered right away by Elizabeth/Maddie. But Elizabeth stared at the audience, then at Adeline, then back at the audience.

"She's forgotten her line!" Mrs. Smith cried backstage. "Where's my script?"

But before Mrs. Smith could find her script, Lara whispered out Adeline's line, straight from her head: "I did see Tom today. He was asking about you."

Maddie's head twitched.

Lara repeated the line.

Then, just like when Daddy's truck has to start slow

on a cold morning, Maddie's brain caught. She opened her mouth, and the words sputtered out. "I did see Tom today. He was asking about you."

After that, the scene went off smooth as packed snow.

But I still got that sled-sliding-down-the-hill feeling because this was not a very good start to our play, if you asked me.

My part started at the very ending of the first act. I stood offstage, and my stomach got sicker and sicker the closer and closer the play got to my part.

"Break a leg, Caroline!" Lara said, popping up behind me as quiet as if she'd floated there.

I turned around and saw that smile and forgot all about being on that sliding-down sled. "Thanks," I said, trying to give back a piece of that smile because I hadn't used my own smile in a long time, I think.

"That's your cue," Lara said.

I ran out onto that stage. At first I couldn't see because of the bright lights there. Then my eyes started seeing. I saw rows and rows of people sitting on folding chairs, waiting on me to say my lines.

And then I saw Luke. He was in the very back row in the very farthest-over chair. But he was there. My little big brother was there to see me.

I walked front and center, where Hamlet the Pig was waiting with five of Sara's little piggies. "There you are, Hamlet," I said. And just like another Laney was on the inside of me, she said all her lines loud and clear and exactly like they ought to have been, according to that *Fair Day* script.

There was one strange minute during that time on-stage, and I didn't think of it until later. Only I'm telling you about that minute now because that's more chronological. I thought I saw a spiderweb, or part of a web, hanging down from that stage ceiling. And the funny thing is that I thought I saw a pig in it. But that picture was in my head for less than a flash, like a school-picture flash on school-picture day. And most of me was being Caroline saying her lines. So I didn't even think about that picture until later on. And I wish I had.

17

The Return of
Climax: Climax II

You shouldn't be confused about having this other chapter called "Climax." There really aren't two of these climaxes. There's one, and I'm right in the middle of that.

Only if you noticed, there are chapters in this book. And books do that so you can stop reading and go to the bathroom or get a drink or maybe go out to recess, and then find your way back to where you left off in your book. Only that last chapter on climax was taking too long, and so I made this one. And that's all there is to that.

Only maybe that's not all there is to that. Because I'm having me a lot of trouble getting to what happened next. And so maybe that's part of it.

Acts 2 and 3 of *Fair Day* went off pretty good. I think not so good as in dress rehearsal, but pretty good for fourth grade. The people in the folding chairs clapped and laughed mostly at the right places.

There were some scary times, with kids forgetting their lines. But not Ms. Connolly and not Mrs. Smith had to look at their scripts to help those kids that forgot. Why? Because Lara Phelps had that whole script with everybody's parts up in her head. When somebody messed up or forgot a line, Lara was there to get them back onto the right words. She did that for all these people:

Maddie
Carlos
Roger
Brianna
Tamara
2 unnamed girls
1 unnamed boy

The only reason I'm not on that list is because Lara had taught me how to learn all my lines by making them into poem songs. So I didn't forget anything.

Right before Act 3, when there was nothing going on, which is called intermission, I peeked through those curtains to see if Luke was still in that chair, and he was. I wondered if he liked Caroline and thought I did a good job as her.

"Did they come?" a voice behind me asked.

I turned to see Lara smiling at me.

"Luke came," I told her. "He's my brother."

"That's great, Laney," she said.

"Yeah." That's what I said because it really did feel like great.

After intermission, I got to be Caroline again, only at the fair, instead of on the farm. Right before I was about to go onstage, I just happened to see Joey Gilbert a ways off. And there was a funny thing about him. Before the play started, Joey reminded me of a balloon blown up so big it could bust. He ran around backstage more than Eric Radabaugh, shouting orders louder than Wayne Wilson himself. But as our play kept going on, I could have sworn on my middle big brother's eyes that something was wrong with Joey

Gilbert. He looked more and more like the air was leaking out of his balloon. I admit that I didn't think so much about this as I'm making out now. This is because I know now what was about to happen. And I guess I've put off telling you as long as I can, with a whole extra chapter.

Our play got over, and all of us actors lined up at the front of the stage and took a big bow, just like we did at dress rehearsal, when nobody was clapping. We did this three times because people in folding chairs were clapping like crazy. And each time I stood up from this bow, I looked back at Luke, and I think he was clapping like everybody else, but it was hard to see with all those lights. I remember that I had this thought. And that was that this could be the happiest I had ever felt in my whole life.

Just like in dress rehearsal, Mrs. Smith said, "And thanks to our backstage crew. Without them, our play couldn't have succeeded."

The audience applauded even louder then, and everybody who'd made signs or scenery or anything stepped up and made a line while we all stepped back.

Lara Phelps was in the exact middle of the stage, and this was on account of Joey telling everybody where they should stand. I felt real good about this, too, because people were clapping for Lara, and she had worked harder than anybody. And I even thought it was a good thing that they were clapping for Joey Gilbert.

That's when I noticed that Joey was not in this line.

I got a chill going down my back, just like if I had been on that sled sliding downhill. I looked to both sides of backstage. Joey stood at one end, and Roger Steeby at the other. Roger was waving wildly to Joey and shouting, "Now! Do it now!"

Joey, he looked like he'd eaten bad mushrooms and was feeling it. But he grabbed a rope, or a string, and I'm not sure about that part, and he pulled.

I heard Roger Steeby shout something. And just like that, all the stage crew on the left side of Lara stepped left, and all on the right stepped right. And this left Lara Phelps standing front and center, larger than life. And faster than you can shout, "Break a leg!" down came things from the ceiling.

These things were balloons and pigs.

I saw the balloons first because they sank like rocks, instead of floating like balloons ought to. Then I saw cardboard pigs fall, too. And Sara's small, stuffed pigs.

Only the balloons hit first. They slapped the floor at Lara's feet. Water shot up. All around the front center of the stage came the *plop, splash, smack* of balloons crashing.

And there was Lara.

Lara covered her head like she was under a bomb attack. One balloon hit her arm and bounced off.

She screamed. Lara screamed.

She got wetter and wetter, until she was as wet as she could get.

I looked up to see if the balloons were done falling and crashing. And I saw a sign hanging above Lara, and this sign was crooked. What it said was this:

FAIR DAY PIG WASH — FREE PIG BATH TODAY!

I remember thinking that that sign was probably supposed to be funny.

And there was Lara.

The cardboard pigs lay on the ground, stuck to the wet floor. They looked dead, like on a cartoon when something gets run over and turns flat. Sara's pigs had skidded in puddles of water and lay scattered over the stage.

And there was Lara.

She was shaking.

When the first pigs and balloons fell, the crowd laughed, like they thought it was all part of the show. Then when the balloons hit Lara and soaked Lara and still more balloons fell, the laughing stopped. Then other sounds, sicky sounds, sprung up, groans and the like.

I think Ms. Connolly was screaming something. I think Mrs. Smith was sobbing. I think I didn't move or do anything or scream or cry.

But there was Lara.

Then it was quiet.

Over. In a way. Nobody moved. Nobody went to Lara. I heard water drip from her head to the stage floor. Still nobody moved. It felt like we were all stuck in one of those frozen moments. I wanted it to be over. I wanted it not to have happened.

And there was Lara. Larger than life.

She turned and looked toward stage left, to Joey Gilbert. Then stage right, to Roger. Then she looked at us. Slowly. To all of us, one by one. And I couldn't tell, when that gaze came to me, I couldn't tell if she was sad for her or sad for us. And maybe with mad mixed in there, too. And there weren't any words she could have shouted at us what would have been louder than her eyes and her lips that were pressed into a straight line and not smiling.

And that's when she did what she did.

Lara Phelps stood herself up straight and turned back to the audience. She smoothed down her wet dress that was stuck to her. She pushed her wet hair out of her face. From where I stood, I watched her smile creep back, slowly, in starts and stops, sputtering kind of, like a drowning person who gets the water pumped out of him so as he can breathe again. She shuffled up to where that microphone still was. And clear as the Fourth of July, she began.

"We ask you to forgive us—"

But she stopped. She stared down at her wet hands. Then she tried again.

"We ask you to be kind. . ." Her voice was soft, so as everybody on both sides of that stage leaned in, straining to hear her.

"Forgiving others instantly—"

She stopped again. I wanted to help. I wanted to shout out rhymes for her: *Kind . . . Find! Bind! Blind! Behind! Peace of Mind!*

She didn't finish. The whole gym was silent. The only sound was a laugh from Joey Gilbert. But that laugh sounded like somebody broke it in two and twisted it up all weird. I looked around our stage and saw Sara Rivers crying. And there were other kids crying, too. But this is something I can't say for sure because I couldn't see so good.

Then Lara was not there.

The curtain came down, and I think it was Lara herself who pulled that curtain because the rest of us hadn't moved. One by one, kids drifted away, not saying "bye" or "see you" to each other.

I wanted to get far away from that place. I wanted Luke. I ran to the curtain and peered out to where Luke had been sitting. Only he wasn't there.

And that sled crashed all the way down.

Tears burned in my throat, clear down to my stomach. I turned back and ran across the stage, down the back steps, and out through that back door that goes to my secret step, where Lara had taught me about poem songs. Only I didn't stop there. I kept running. Down the step, around the bushes, around the school building.

. . . And smack into somebody.

My brain wanted it to be Joey Gilbert so I could beat on him until one of us couldn't stand up. I swung at the person in the dark, believing I was hitting Joey, making him hurt.

"Laney." The voice was quiet. Hands held my wrists and kept my fists from landing. "It's okay, Laney."

I looked up into the big brown eyes of my brother Luke.

"You did good, Laney. So did she. You did us proud." That was what Luke said to me.

I burst into tears, like a balloon breaking open its sides. I cried and cried on my littlest big brother's shoulder. And he didn't push me away or call me a big, fat baby.

My daddy says there's no such things as miracles, but I say he is wrong. I do believe in those miracles, of which this was one.

18
Resolution

I warned you right up front in chapter one that this story might not turn out as good as a made-up story, where you can put in the happy-ever-after parts. Mrs. Smith says stories have resolutions. A resolution is what happens at the end, where things get solved. That word, *resolution*, almost has *solve* inside of it. And this makes me think of a play inside of a play, which is what you get in that Shakespeare story called *Hamlet*. It was a play its own self, but in that play they were putting on a play. And that can give me the chills if I think about it too much.

But like I said, this story doesn't get all solved in the end. And I'm sorry about that, but that's just the way it is. And you can't say I didn't warn you.

But here is what happened next. Most of this action happened without me. But here is what I know anyway.

- Principal Russell got real mad at all of the whole entire fourth grade. She was a dead man's eyelash away from kicking all of us out of Paris Elementary on account of ruining the play, the wood floor on the stage, and a whole lot of other things besides that.
- On Saturday, Principal Russell and Lara and Lara's parents had a very serious talk in the principal's office. Lara's parents swore like sailors on leave and said they knew something like this was going to happen.
- Principal Russell tried to make Lara tell who dumped water and pigs and balloons on her in the play.
- They tried really, really hard to make her do this.
- Lara did not do this.
- Principal Russell said Lara had to tell what she knew—or else. Lara chose "or else."

- Finally, Principal Russell got so mad that even though she and Lara and Lara's parents and everybody else in Paris, Missouri, knew Lara hadn't done one thing wrong, she "had no other recourse." And that's where the stories get mixed up because I don't know about everybody else, but I had no idea what *recourse* meant.
- Some kids were saying that the principal kicked Lara out of Paris Elementary. Some were saying that Lara got a bunch of detentions, which is the opposite of getting kicked out because you stay even longer. I don't know if either of these parts is true or maybe neither one.
- Lara's parents got madder at Principal Russell and Paris Elementary than Principal Russell and Paris Elementary got at Lara or anybody else.

This was the gossip I knew before going to school on Monday.

On Monday when I got to school, not only was Lara not there, her special-made desk wasn't there, too.

"Where's Lara?" I asked, glancing back at the door, where she'd first walked in.

"She's gone." Mrs. Smith's voice sounded funny, and she wouldn't look up from her desk.

"Where'd she go?" Sara asked.

"Where's her desk?" Eric asked.

"She's gone. And she's not coming back." Mrs. Smith took a big breath of air. And that was when I noticed it. The air had changed back to like it was before Lara appeared in that doorway of our classroom.

"That's not fair!" I blurted out. "They can't kick *her* out of school! She didn't do anything."

"Lara didn't get kicked out of school," Mrs. Smith said quietly, looking up now, with red eyes. "Her parents have decided it would be best to move Lara to a different school, a private school in St. Louis, I think."

Joey Gilbert stayed quiet as a stuffed pig, and Eric Radabaugh seemed frozen to his desk.

"Will she come to class again? To say good-bye?" Theresa asked.

I glanced over at Theresa. She looked like she had when her cat, Fiji, died.

"Lara won't leave without saying good-bye, will she?" Amanda asked.

"I packed up her things and left them in the office," Mrs. Smith said. "Her parents will collect her belongings on their way out of town today."

I wanted to shout that it wasn't fair again. That of all of us, Lara was the one who should be staying. But I didn't say nothing more. Neither did anybody. We sat in our desks not saying nothing for a long time.

Finally, Mrs. Smith stood up and came around the front of her desk and sat on it. "Do you children understand what you did to Lara?"

The only answers were choking sounds and crying noises.

"Do you understand what Lara did for you?" Mrs. Smith asked this very quietly. Then she answered it. "Lara Phelps took all the blame for you."

You'd have thought that somebody'd died, instead of moved away. That's how silent it was in our room. I thought about when Lara showed up that first day and how you could have heard a pin or a feather drop if you'd have had one. And this was quieter than that.

Joey Gilbert was the first one to speak. "Why would she do that?"

My mind flashed me a picture of Lara, standing on stage, larger than life, water dripping from her elbows and shoulders and hair. I saw how that smile worked its way back up to her mouth. And I could hear her stumbling over the words of a rhyming poem she wanted to give to the audience. Only this time I heard her saying it to me. So I said it along with her, out loud, in our classroom:

> "We ask you to forgive us.
> We ask you to be kind.
> Forgiving others instantly. . ."

I finished that poem in my head, making it say: *Forgiving others instantly will give you peace of mind.* Only I couldn't get that part out in time because my throat got clogged up.

There were sniffles and sobs and crying noises going on all over the room now. And some of these were coming from Joey Gilbert.

Then Joey got up from his desk and walked over to the same worktable where he'd drawn all those pigs.

We watched Joey. I think Mrs. Smith started to tell him to sit down, but she must have changed her mind.

Joey picked up a marker and started writing on a poster board. The marker's squeak sounded like a fire alarm. He stopped. "How do you spell *trick?*" he asked.

Mrs. Smith told him.

I got up and went over so as I could see that poster board. Joey had written onto it: I AM SORRY THAT WE DID THAT TRICK.

He turned around and frowned at me. "Laney, help. I don't know how to rhyme. What rhymes with *trick?*"

I took the marker he held out to me.

"*Sick?*" Amanda suggested, coming over to the table.

"*Quick?*" Wayne shouted.

Desks were emptying as everybody came to the table.

"How about *pick?*" Maddie said.

Below Joey's line, "I am sorry that we did that trick," I wrote: ON LARA PHELPS WE WILL NEVER PICK.

"Good job, Laney!" Eric Radabaugh shouted, bumping the table, but just on accident.

"I want to do one!" Sara shouted, pulling out another poster board.

"Sara!" Maddie cried.

"What, Maddie?" Sara fired back.

"I'll help you."

"Me, too!" Wayne shouted louder.

Pretty soon the worktable was full of poster boards. Markers squealed and squeaked. Kids fired spelling questions at Mrs. Smith.

There were signs that said:

PLEASE DON'T SAY THAT THIS IS THE END.
LARA, WILL YOU BE OUR FRIEND?

DOING THAT TO YOU WAS A MEAN ATTACK.
IF I COULD I'D TAKE IT BACK.

THANKS FOR FORGIVING US.
EVEN THOUGH WE ARE A MUSS.

WE WERE STUPID AND WE WERE MEAN.
YOU WERE THE NICEST PERSON
THAT WE HAVE EVER SEEN.

I watched this and saw it with my own eyes. And it felt real good to see this part of all of us, the good-sign-making part. And I wondered if Lara had seen it first, this good-sign-making part, under all the bad-sign-making part. And it felt like maybe the air in our classroom was changing back again.

"Oh no! There she is! They're leaving!" Mrs. Smith was standing at the window, pointing. "Her parents are heading to the car with her things! There! Isn't that Lara in the backseat?"

I ran over to the window and looked. It was Lara, taking up the whole backseat of the blue minivan. "We have to catch her!" I screamed. "Can we—?"

"Run!" Mrs. Smith shouted. She had taught us the school rules about not running in the school or the halls. But she said it again. "Run! Hurry!"

Kids grabbed their signs and raced out of the room. But I didn't have a sign. I *had* to have a sign for Lara. I grabbed the last blank poster and wrote in huge letters:

THANKS!

Then I ran to catch up with everybody.

When I got outside, I joined the line of kids on the grass, across the street from the parking lot. Lara's parents were in the van. Lara was looking straight ahead, not seeing us. Or pretending not to see us.

"Lara!" Joey shouted.

"Lara!" Wayne shouted louder.

"She doesn't see us!" Sara cried.

"The exit!" I hollered. If we could get to the exit of the parking lot, they'd *have* to drive by us. Lara would have to see us.

I ran so fast that I dropped my sign and had to pick it up. We raced to the exit, shouting all the way. We got there, just before that van pulled up.

Then Joey shouted, "Lara!" And he held up his sign.

And pretty soon our whole entire fourth-grade class of Paris Elementary was yelling her name and waving signs. "Lara! Lara! Lara!"

Lara's car took the exit. It drove by slowly.

Lara turned. Her chubby palms pressed against the window. Her face pushed at the glass, taking up the whole, entire space. Her little smile got bigger and bigger, larger than life even, as her gaze moved from sign to sign.

I held up my sign that only said THANKS! on it and hoped it was good enough. I wished it could have had THANKS FOR LUKE in it. I wished it could have been a poem song that rhymed. I knew right then that Lara Phelps was going to play in my head like one of those songs that won't never leave your brain, but they just keep playing. She saw stuff. And I was going to try to see stuff, too. Everywhere I'd go for the rest of my life, she'd be there, larger than life. Larger-than-life Lara. Only I didn't say any of that on my sign, except THANKS.

But when Lara's gaze got to my sign, I could tell she liked it. Her smile pressed against that window. And I wanted her dad to stop that car. I wanted Lara to get out and come back to class with us.

Only I figured she had her places to go. There had to be a lot of elementaries what needed a Larger-than-life Lara in them.

And then that blue van drove off, with dust puffing from the back of it. We stood there, still holding our signs up, even after you couldn't see that van anymore.

Mrs. Smith, she says that when your story is over, you shouldn't keep going on and on about stuff you thought of since that story happened. If somebody has stuck with your story the whole entire way through, then you just got to let them go.

"When your story is over," says Mrs. Smith, "it's over." And I figure she's right, and that's just the way it is.